The HARDY BOYS *Mystery Stories*
BY FRANKLIN W. DIXON

"CLEAR OUT OF HERE," CAPTAIN ROYAL STORMED,
"AND DON'T LET ME CATCH YOU AROUND HERE
AGAIN!"

The Secret of the Caves

HARDY BOYS MYSTERY STORIES

THE SECRET OF THE CAVES

By

FRANKLIN W. DIXON

NEW YORK

GROSSET & DUNLAP

PUBLISHERS

Printed in the United States of America

CONTENTS

iv   Contents

THE HARDY BOYS:
THE SECRET OF THE CAVES

CHAPTER I

OVERBOARD

"WELL, the stealing of autos in this neighborhood has come to an end, Frank. Wonder if anybody will ever take to stealing motorboats."

"Perhaps, Joe. But there isn't the chance to steal a boat that there was to steal cars."

"Gee, now that the excitement is over I wonder what will come up next."

"Don't know; but something is bound to happen sooner or later—it always does."

"Hope it comes soon—I don't want to get rusty."

It was a Saturday afternoon in June, one of those warm, drowsy days when even the leaves of the trees seem too indolent to stir. There was scarcely a ripple on the surface of

1

the water, no movement but the flow of the incoming tide.

Three motorboats circled lazily about in Barmet Bay within sight of the city of Bayport. The lazy spirit of the afternoon seemed to have spread to the occupants of the boats, for they lounged about in comfortable attitudes.

Biff Hooper, in his craft, the *Envoy*, had devised a way of steering with his foot while sprawled on the side cushions.

In a motorboat close by, the *Napoli*, sat Tony Prito, whose dark hair, olive skin, and sparkling eyes indicated his Italian parentage even more emphatically than his name. In the third craft were two lads who need no introduction to readers of previous volumes in this series.

The boy at the wheel, a tall, dark, handsome lad of about sixteen, was Frank Hardy, and the other, a fair, curly-headed fellow about a year his junior, was his brother Joe. These boys were the sons of Fenton Hardy, an internationally famous private detective who lived in Bayport.

"I didn't expect to see you fellows out on the bay this afternoon," shouted Biff Hooper, raising his head over the side of his boat.

"Where did you think we'd be?" called back Frank. "Up in the attic, studying?"

"Thought you'd be out in your car," and Biff grinned widely.

There was a laugh from Tony Prito, and the Hardy boys also laughed with great good-humor. Their car was a standing joke among their chums, and, as Chet Morton put it, "standing" joke described it exactly, for it seldom moved.

"Never mind," returned Joe. "That old car served its purpose, anyway. We used it only as bait."

"It was mighty good bait," said Tony. "You caught some big fish with that old crate."

"It has earned its keep," Frank called back. "We're going to put it on a pension and let it stay in our garage for the rest of its life, without charge."

The boys were referring to a roadster that the Hardy lads had purchased out of their savings some time previous. It was a car that proved the old axiom that beauty is only skin deep, for although it glittered with nickel and paint and although its lines were trim and smooth, its inner workings were utterly beyond the comprehension of Bayport mechanics. For a few weeks after its purchase the car ran, eccentrically enough, but still it ran. Then, one day, for no apparent reason, it gave up the ghost and no amount of tinkering would prompt it even to move out of the garage.

However, as Joe had said, the car had served its purpose. The boys had picked it up cheaply, with a definite object in view. As told in the preceding volume of this series, "The Hardy Boys: The Shore Road Mystery," there had been a series of mysterious automobile thefts on the Shore Road leading out of Bayport, numerous pleasure cars and trucks having been stolen, and no amount of investigation on the part of the police had succeeded in revealing their whereabouts or the identity of the thieves.

Frank and Joe Hardy, who had earned considerable local fame by their activities as amateur detectives, in emulation of their famous father, had decided to lay a trap for the automobile thieves and, buying the gorgeous rattletrap, parked it on the Shore Road for several nights, concealing themselves in the rear. After many adventures, the Hardy boys captured the thieves and recovered the stolen cars. They collected several handsome rewards for their work, so their investment in the roadster proved exceedingly profitable after all.

"The car owners around Bayport have sure been breathing easier since that affair was cleared up," said Biff.

"I don't think there'll be any more car thieving for a long time," Tony declared. "The two sleuths here put a stop to that."

"We had a good time doing it," Frank admitted. "I'm rather sorry it's all over."

"Never satisfied!" commented Biff.

He prodded the wheel with his foot and the *Envoy* swung about with its nose pointing down the bay. Barmet Bay, three miles long, opened on the Atlantic, and in the distance the boys could see a motor yacht that ran daily between Bayport and one of the towns on the coast, a trim little passenger craft that was proceeding toward them at a fast clip.

"Where are you going?" shouted Tony.

"Out to meet the passenger boat."

"Race you!"

"So will we!" called Frank.

Biff abandoned his indolent posture and settled down to take advantage of his head start. His boat leaped ahead with a roar. Tony Prito had to make a half turn before he could get under way.

The Hardy boys were similarly unprepared, but they had no doubt of the ability of the *Sleuth* to overhaul Biff's boat quickly. Their craft was one of the speediest in the bay, with smooth lines and a powerful engine.

They had trouble on the turn, for the swells of the other boats caught the *Sleuth* and put it off its course, and by the time the craft was nosing in pursuit, Biff Hooper had a good lead and Tony Prito was also ahead of them.

"Step on it!" said Joe.

Frank "stepped on it," and the *Sleuth* began eating up the intervening distance. Rocking and swaying, prow well out of the water, the boat overhauled the *Napoli* and Frank grinned at Tony as they crept by. The Italian lad was getting every ounce of speed of which his engine was capable and although he jockeyed to try to put the Hardy boys off the course, they sped on and soon left him behind.

Biff had been tinkering with the engine of his craft and had evidently made a few improvements, for the *Envoy* was going along at a clip it had never before achieved.

"Looks as if he intends to put one over on us," muttered Frank, as he opened up the engine to the last notch. "He'll beat us to the boat at this rate."

The motor yacht was about a mile away.

On through the water plunged the *Sleuth,* gaining slowly but surely on the craft ahead.

Once in a while Biff cast a hasty glance backward to wave mockingly at them. He misjudged an approaching wave on one of these occasions and the *Envoy* swerved; he lost valuable seconds righting the craft into its course again and the *Sleuth* gained.

The yacht was about a quarter of a mile distant when the *Sleuth* at last pulled up beside the other boat. Inch by inch it forged ahead until the bow of each boat was on a line with the other. Then the *Sleuth's* greater speed became manifest as it pulled away, leaving Biff shaking his head in exasperation.

Suddenly Joe, who had been looking at the passenger yacht in the distance, gave a shout of alarm.

"Look!" he cried.

Frank glanced up just in time to see an immense puff of black smoke bursting from above the deck of the yacht. Then, across the waves, was borne to their ears the roar of an explosion.

They could see figures running about on the deck of the boat. One of them, a woman, ran directly to the rail and began to clamber up on it.

"What on earth—" gasped Joe.

"She's going overboard!"

Another figure ran out, making a frantic grab at the woman who was balanced perilously on top of the rail. Then, her arms outspread, the woman jumped. The boys saw her plunge down the side of the yacht, and there was a splash as she hurtled into the water.

A moment later she emerged and they could see her swimming about and waving her arms. The *Sleuth* had drawn closer to the yacht in the meantime and now the boys could hear a faint cry for help.

Tensely, Frank leaned over the wheel. Great clouds of smoke were pouring from the yacht.

"We'll have to rescue her!" he said. "It's her only chance."

The yacht had passed the woman by now, and although a life-buoy had been flung out it was some distance away from her. Hampered by her wet clothes, the woman was making no progress toward it. Slowly, the yacht began to circle, but the lads saw that it would never reach her in time.

The *Sleuth* ploughed on through the waves.

The boys saw the woman throw up her hands with a despairing gesture and disappear beneath the surface.

CHAPTER II

The Rescue

As the Hardy boys sped toward the woman, who appeared above the surface again in a moment and began to struggle wildly, they saw that confusion prevailed on board the yacht.

Great clouds of smoke were pouring from amidship. People were running frantically about the deck. Efforts were being made to lower a lifeboat, but apparently something went wrong, for it sagged perilously and then stuck, with two sailors working hastily to release it.

But the boys' immediate concern was the woman. She disappeared beneath the water again and they were fearful that she had gone under for the last time. Then, as the *Sleuth* surged forward, they saw her emerge once more. They were close enough now to see her frightened face, and, as the *Sleuth* sped within a few yards of her, Joe poised himself and dived.

He plunged into the water just as the wo-

man was going down for the third time. He
kept cool and, remembering the first aid in-
struction he had received, took care not **to**
come within reach of the wildly clutching hands.
He grasped the woman by the hair and then,
keeping behind her, managed to get a grip
that did not endanger himself. Had she been
able to throw her arms about him, he would
have been dragged beneath the surface
with her.

Joe struggled toward the *Sleuth*. It had sped
past when he dived, but Frank had quickly
brought the craft around and Joe had to
swim but a few strokes. Frank throttled
down the engine and he was able to give a
hand in assisting the woman on board. She
was dragged into the boat, dripping and almost unconscious, and Joe clung to the gun-
wale until Frank grasped his shoulders and
hauled him over the side.

In the meantime, the Hardy boys' chums
were speeding toward the yacht. The race
was forgotten.

Frank and Joe did their best to revive the
half-conscious woman. Her immersion in the
water and the shock of being face to face with
death had left her weakened, and she was
moaning and murmuring as she lay on the cushions. Joe gave what first aid he could, moving
her arms back and forth to restore circulation.

while Frank set the course of the *Sleuth* in the direction of the yacht.

Biff Hooper had already reached the passenger boat. He drew up alongside, with Tony Prito, in the *Envoy,* not far behind. Passengers were crowding to the rail, some shouting and screaming with fright, some pleading to be taken off.

Biff and Tony were ready to offer their boats for this purpose, but they noticed that the cloud of smoke had diminished in volume. A uniformed man was bellowing through a megaphone.

"No danger!" he roared. "The fire is under control!"

But it was plain that many in the crowd were afraid there would be another explosion.

"Take us off!" screeched a wild-eyed woman. "Take us off before the boat blows up!"

She scrambled up on the rail, but the uniformed man seized her and prevented her from trying to leap overboard.

"Need any help?" shouted Biff.

"Stand by for a while," returned the officer. "We're getting this fire under control but we don't know how bad it is."

Biff and Tony, in their motorboats, cruised in the neighborhood of the yacht, as the ship's officer asked. The passengers were milling about on deck, badly frightened, but gradually they became calmer as a steward assured them that there was no danger. The heavy cloud of smoke decreased in volume. The boat's crew was small and the fire-fighting equipment was limited, but in a little while it became evident that the blaze was not as bad as it had seemed and that it had indeed been checked in time.

Soon the smoke cloud ceased rolling up from below.

The uniformed man came on deck again with a megaphone. He raised it to his lips and bellowed:

"Thanks, boys, but we won't need you."

"That's fine!" shouted Tony, in reply. "Fire all out?"

"Tin of gasoline exploded. It didn't spread much. We'll be able to make Bayport under our own power."

"Righto!" called Biff. "We're going in now, anyway. If you need us, give us a hail."

"We'll do that."

The motorboats circled away. In the distance, Biff and Tony could see the Hardy boys in the *Sleuth,* with the woman they had rescued.

"Your passenger is all right!" shouted Biff, to the captain. "Our chums will bring her back with them."

He turned the nose of his craft toward the *Sleuth*.

The Hardy boys were doing their best to revive the woman they had rescued from the waves.

She was not unconscious but she seemed very weak and scarcely appeared to realize where she was.

She was an elderly woman, dressed in black, and although her immersion in the water had undoubtedly been a tremendous shock, the boys could see that she was of an exceedingly nervous temperament and evidently not in the best of health, for she was worn and pale.

"Where am I?" she moaned. "Where am I now?"

"You're quite safe," Frank assured her. "You're in a motorboat."

"You saved me?"

"We got you out of the water just in time."

"I want to go to Bayport," said the woman weakly.

"We'll take you there," promised Joe. "It isn't very far away. We will take you there at once."

"I want to go to Bayport," she repeated. "It's important. I have to see some one there."

"Head the boat around, Frank," said Joe

quietly. He had seen their chums returning from the neighborhood of the yacht, so he realized that there was no further danger from the fire.

"I must be in Bayport to-night," gasped the woman. "I must go there to see Fenton Hardy —the detective."

Then she collapsed weakly, her eyes closed, and she was a dead weight in Joe's arms. She had fainted.

The Hardy boys looked at one another in astonishment.

"She wants to see dad!" exclaimed Frank incredulously.

It was a strange coincidence that they, of all people, should have rescued her when she was on her way to see their father.

Fenton Hardy had many clients, some of whom came long distances to consult him. He was one of the greatest private detectives in the country and his fame was widespread. He had been for many years on the New York force and had finally achieved his ambition of setting up an agency of his own. He had moved to Bayport, on the Atlantic coast, with his family and his success had been immediate. He had successfully handled many difficult cases and his services were much in demand.

Frank and Joe Hardy, his sons, were anxious to follow in their father's footsteps, in spite of his objections and in spite of their mother's desire that they prepare themselves for medicine and law respectively. But the boys had a natural deductive bent and they had taken several local cases on their own initiative, succeeding so well that Fenton Hardy had finally withdrawn his objections and agreed that if, when they were of age, they still desired to become private investigators, he would not stand in their way.

The Hardy boys were introduced in the first volume of this series entitled, "The Hardy Boys: The Tower Treasure," wherein they handled their first case of any consequence. A large quantity of bonds and jewels had been stolen from an old mansion on the outskirts of Bayport and after numerous adventures the lads traced the loot and ran the criminal to earth. Other volumes of the series have recounted their adventures in handling other cases that came their way, all of which they successfully solved.

In the volume immediately preceding the present book, entitled, "The Hardy Boys: The Shore Road Mystery," the lads, as already mentioned, rounded up a gang of automobile thieves who had stolen a number of cars and trucks from points along the Shore Road above Barmet Bay. After that, things had been quiet around Bayport and the boys were beginning to think that mysteries were at a discount.

"We'd better get her back to Bayport right away," said Joe, as he looked down at the unconscious woman. "She may be dying."

"Splash some water on her face. She's just fainted, I think."

Joe rendered impromptu aid, but the woman was in a dead faint and he could not revive her at all.

In the meantime, the motorboat was heading back in the direction of the city. Frank had "let her out" to the utmost and the speedy craft was eating up the distance. He crouched tensely at the wheel, and sheets of spray splashed over the bow.

"I wonder what on earth she wants to see dad about," he said to himself. Then he chuckled. "Dad will have to thank us for saving one of his clients."

CHAPTER III

Miss Todd

Frank Hardy lost no time on the run back to Bayport. Instead of proceeding directly to the boathouse, he docked the *Sleuth* at one of the city wharves. There the lads were fortunate enough to find a taxi. The woman was still unconscious when they arrived, so with the assistance of the taxi driver they lifted her out of the boat and into the car.

Frank instructed the man to drive to the office of a doctor they knew well, and there the woman received attention.

"She has evidently been under a great strain," the doctor told them. "The shock of the explosion and her struggle in the water were just the finishing touches."

Under his expert administrations the woman was soon revived sufficiently to sit up. She looked about her.

"What happened?" she asked weakly.

"You are in good hands, madam," the doctor assured her. "Just be quiet for a while and you will be all right."

In a few minutes, the woman had recovered. First of all, she insisted on thanking the boys for rescuing her.

"If it hadn't been for these brave lads I would have been drowned. It was foolish of me to jump off that yacht, but I've been very nervous lately, and when I heard the explosion and saw all that smoke I lost my head completely."

"Well," said the doctor genially, "there's been no harm done. You were on your way to Bayport, weren't you, and here you are."

"Am I in Bayport now?"

"Yes."

"You must take me to Fenton Hardy at once, please," said the woman, sitting up. "I must see him."

"There'll be no trouble about that. These boys are Fenton Hardy's sons."

The woman gazed at the Hardy boys in surprise.

"His sons!" she exclaimed.

"Fenton Hardy is our father," stated Frank.

The woman was evidently astonished.

"Isn't that strange! To think that your father should be the very man I was coming to see "

"He's at home now," said Joe. "As soon as you're feeling well enough we'll take you there."

"That will be good of you. I came to Bayport for the sole purpose of seeing your father."

"Are you coming to visit us?" asked Joe.

The woman shook her head.

"No. I want to see your father on business. Important business. It is private, so I'm afraid I can't tell you any more about it."

The boys forbore to question her.

"I suppose I should tell you my name. I am Miss Evangeline Todd."

They bowed in acknowledgement.

"Will you take me to your father now? I feel much better. I'm very anxious to see him at once. There is no time to lose."

Miss Todd seemed quite agitated, and although the lads felt that a few minutes more or less would make no particular difference, they decided that it would be best to humor her. Miss Todd got to her feet, and although she was still physically weak, she evidently had a mind of her own for she was determined to remain no longer in the doctor's office when she was so near her goal.

Accordingly, the Hardy boys helped her out of the office to the waiting taxi.

During the brief drive she repeatedly expressed her astonishment at having been rescued by the Hardy boys "of all people."

"I've often heard of you boys," she said. "You often help your father, don't you?"

"Whenever we can," laughed Frank.

"Well, I hope you can help him now. I want to learn the truth about poor Todham."

The lads waited expectantly, but the elderly lady said no more about the object of her call. She seemed somewhat eccentric, and muttered to herself a great deal.

"Poor Todham," she repeated, over and over again. "I do hope Mr. Hardy can help me. It's all very strange."

The car drew up at the door of the Hardy home and the boys helped Miss Todd alight. They brought her into the house and their father met them at the door, evidently surprised.

"A client for you, Dad," explained Frank. "We picked her up just a little while ago."

He did not tell his father just how they had "picked up" the elderly woman.

"And is this Fenton Hardy?" said Miss Todd. She grasped the noted detective by the hand. "I've come a long distance to see you. These fine boys of yours saved my life."

"You've been in the water!" exclaimed Mr. Hardy. He called to his wife. "Laura, will you look after this lady and make her comfortable?''

Miss Todd's clothing was not entirely dry, owing to her immersion in the waters of Barmet Bay, and when Mrs. Hardy appeared she insisted on taking the guest upstairs and providing her with a complete change of garments. Miss Todd insisted that her business could not wait, even for such an important detail as dry clothes, but the better counsel of Mrs. Hardy prevailed.

When Miss Todd came downstairs some time later she was still very weak and nervous but in a more settled frame of mind.

"If you'll come into my office," suggested Fenton Hardy, courteously, "I'll be glad to hear your story."

Miss Todd looked around.

"I had intended to keep it private," she said; "but you've all been so kind to me that I'm sure it will do no harm if you all know. That is, if you would care to listen," she added, turning to Mrs. Hardy and the boys.

Both Frank and Joe were very curious to know the nature of the mysterious affair that had brought Miss Todd to Bayport and it did not require any persuasion for them to remain.

Miss Todd sat down in an armchair, and after she was duly settled began a long, rambling narrative.

"It's about my brother," she said. "My twin brother, Todham. He's a very clever man —a professor. Perhaps you've heard of him. Professor Todham Todd, Ph.D. It all started when Todham and I went on that railway journey to visit Cousin Albert. At the time I said that I had a strange feeling that something was going to happen, and perhaps we had better not go, but Todham said I was foolish, so we went. And I was right. It turned out that I was right after all."

"Yes?" said Mr. Hardy encouragingly, wondering to what all this was leading.

"I was quite right," declared Miss Todd emphatically. "Because something *did* happen. There was a wreck. The train jumped off the track. It was a terrible wreck. There were five people killed and it was a blessing Todham and I weren't killed too. But we were hurt. We were badly hurt. I've never felt the same since. My nerves have never been right. As for Todham, he always had been a nervous sort of man, and after that wreck he went all to pieces. The doctor said he would be all right after a while, that all he needed was rest and quiet, and I believed he was right. But we sued the railway for damages."

"Did you win the suit?" asked Mr. Hardy.

"It has not come to trial. The lawyers delayed everything. In the meantime, poor Tod-

ham was acting strangely. You wouldn't think
he was the same man. He was very queer. I
used to wonder if the railway wreck had af-
fected his mind. Instead of getting better, he
became worse. Then one night, just before
the trial was to come off, he disappeared.''

"Disappeared!''

"He walked out of the house one night and
from that minute to this we haven't seen hide
nor hair of him," declared Evangeline Todd.
"We have heard of him, but he's like a will-
o'-the-wisp. We have heard of him in different places, but when we come to look for
him, he's gone. He has never written to us.
There hasn't been any real trace of him. The
shock was too much for me, and I collapsed and
I haven't been well since. Not a bit well. My
nerves have been completely shattered.''

"When did your brother disappear?" asked
the detective.

"Months ago. This happened four months
back.''

Fenton Hardy frowned.

"Four months ago! That makes it more difficult. If you had come to me earlier I would
have had a better chance of helping you.''

"Don't say you won't help me, Mr. Hardy,"
entreated the woman. "Please don't say you
won't take the case.''

"I didn't mean it that way," said the detective kindly. "I meant that the chances of tracing your brother are not as good now as they would have been four months ago. I'll do what I can, of course, but I'm afraid it will be a hard task."

"We searched for him everywhere, Mr. Hardy. I'm sure he is still alive, for we've had reports of him from different places. But I have no idea what can have happened to him."

"It's just possible that he has had a mental breakdown," said the detective. "You say he was acting strangely after the wreck. He may be in a hospital somewhere, and unable to communicate with you."

"I'm quite sure he didn't deliberately run away. Todham has always been so quiet and studious and so anxious to give no trouble to any one. Something dreadful must have happened to him. If it weren't for hearing that he has been seen in these different places, I would believe that he is dead. As it is, I'm sure he is still alive."

"Perhaps we can find some trace of him," said Mr. Hardy. "I'll take the case, Miss Todd, and, although I can't promise to find your brother, you may be sure that I'll do the best I can."

"Thank you. Thank you, Mr. Hardy. I knew you wouldn't refuse. I wish now I had come to you in the first place, instead of wasting so much precious time."

"Perhaps we can recover the lost ground. With a bit of luck, we may be able to pick up his trail."

Miss Todd sank back in her chair.

"Oh, I hope so. I hope so. I have been so worried." She clasped her hands nervously. "Find him for me, Mr. Hardy, and I'll pay you well. I must know what has become of Todham."

Her face suddenly became pale. The strain of the narrative had been too much for her. She relaxed limply.

Mrs. Hardy hurried forward.

"Get me a glass of water, Frank," she said quickly. "She has fainted."

CHAPTER IV

CONCERNING TODHAM TODD

IT WAS quite evident that Miss Todd was in no condition to go to any of the city hotels. She needed rest and quiet more than anything else, and when she had been revived a few minutes later, Mrs. Hardy insisted that she remain in the Hardy home for a few days as a guest. Her sympathy had gone out to the distracted woman, and although at first Evangeline Todd would not consider the proposal, being afraid of imposing on their hospitality, Mr. Hardy insisted that she remain.

"Your story interests me very much," he said. "I'll be very glad to take the case, on one condition."

"What condition is that?"

"On condition that you accept our invitation to stay here for a while until you are feeling better."

So Evangeline Todd was prevailed upon to stay and Fenton Hardy at once prepared to take up the trail of the missing professor. He had no important cases in hand at the time, so he was able to spare a few days for preliminary investigation work and he decided that his best plan was to go directly to the college town where the Todds had their home.

"Sometimes a professional, and a stranger, can pick up clues that wouldn't fall in the way of a police detective who is known in the town," he said. "I'll run up there and see what I can discover."

Mr. Hardy was accustomed to being called out of town suddenly and the family were used to his abrupt departures. The detective was a man who acted quickly, once he had made a decision, and Miss Todd was surprised to see him leaving immediately.

"No use wasting any time," he explained cheerfully, having paused only long enough to pack a bag with a few essentials. "I'll get busy at once."

Although Frank and Joe Hardy were curious to learn further details of the latest mystery on which their father was working, and in which they had taken a small part, Miss Todd had evidently suffered more from her adventure in Barmet Bay than they had at first thought. She was obliged to keep to her room over Sunday and the lads had no chance to talk to her, as Mrs. Hardy decided that their guest should not be disturbed. Wisely, Mrs.

Hardy wanted to keep the woman's mind off the matter of her brother's disappearance and she knew that if the boys beseiged her with questions her state of anxiety would be only rendered worse.

On Monday, when the boys returned to school, they were met at the gate by Chet Morton, heading a group of grinning chums. Chet, a plump, jovial youth, equally fond of food and fun, held up a restraining hand.

"We would fain talk with thee, noble youths," he said. "Humble varlets though we are, we would crave your indulgence for a time."

"You sound like Shakespeare or somebody," said Joe.

"Probably somebody," Chet agreed. "Young masters, we have gathered here to-day to do honor to two brave and bright young men whom we are proud to call our chums. Perhaps," he went on, in the manner of an orator, "in the years to come, when we are poor and unnoticed people, we may be able to say to our grandchildren that once upon a time we went to school with the Hardy boys, that we went swimming with them, and that they often gave us rides in their motorboat. However, that is not getting to the point—"

"What's it all about?" asked Frank. "What's all this speech for?"

"Patience. Patience. Our little committee has waited patiently for your arrival and now we wish to show you our esteem and regard. It has come to our notice that on Saturday, the fourteenth instant, you did bravely, heroically, and nobly perform the humane act of hauling an old lady out of the water when she had swallowed several gallons of Barmet Bay and was in grave danger of drowning. As a slight token of our appreciation we wish you to accept these little tokens—" here Chet gestured to Biff Hooper, who grinned and stepped forward with two shiny objects on an old cushion—"not so much for their intrinsic value, which is considerable, but for the spirit in which they are meant."

Chet took a deep breath.

"I don't know whether that's all quite correct," he said, "but I learned some of it from a book."

Then, very gravely, he picked up the shiny objects, which proved to be impromptu medals carved from the tops of tin biscuit boxes, dangling from red ribbons, and pinned one on the chest of each of the Hardy boys.

There were loud cheers and shrieks of laughter from the boys at this mock ceremony, and the Hardy boys joined in the laugh as well. However, behind all the nonsense, the lads realized that their chums were proud of them. The tin medals were embarrassing, and the boys watched for their first opportunity to take them off.

"Seriously," said Chet, some time later when he was alone with the brothers, "the fellows think you did some mighty smart work fishing that lady out of the water. The captain of the boat told people about it when the yacht docked."

"We couldn't very well stand by and watch her drown," said Frank. "If Biff and Tony could have got there first they'd have done the same."

"Sure! But the point is, you chaps got there first and saved her life. If you hadn't been there, Biff and Tony couldn't have done very much, for their boats aren't fast enough. Where is the lady now? Did she give you her name?"

Frank and Joe then told Chet about Miss Evangeline Todd and about the coincidence that her visit to Bayport had been with the object of seeing Fenton Hardy. Chet was greatly interested when they told him about her search for the missing professor.

"A professor missing, eh? That's something new. If one of the professor's students had disappeared there wouldn't be much mystery about it. I know one student of this high school who would like to drop out of sight for a while—until after these exams are over, at any rate.''

"You're hopeless,'' laughed Frank, and just then the opening bell rang, cutting off further conversation.

When the boys returned home at noon they found that Miss Todd had recovered sufficiently to come downstairs. She seemed in much better spirits and the rest had evidently done her a great deal of good, because she was not in the highly nervous state of the previous Saturday.

"It's such a relief to know that the case is in good hands,'' she said. "If Fenton Hardy can't find poor Todham, I'm sure no one can. Though he may turn up of his own accord,'' she added.

"We'll hope for the best,'' said Mrs. Hardy quietly.

"Dad didn't like to question you too much on Saturday,'' Frank remarked. "He didn't want to bother you more than he could help.''

"I'm afraid I wasn't in any condition to tell him many details.''

"Perhaps if you would tell us anything you overlooked, we might be able to help out a little, too.''

Miss Todd was thoughtful for a moment.

"There were a few things about Todham that would identify him almost anywhere,'' she said.

"For instance, he was very careless about his shoes."

"His shoes?" echoed the boys.

"He *would* not keep them laced. It was simply impossible to keep an eye on that man, and if I didn't watch him he was just as likely as not to go out to classes in the morning with his shoelaces dragging on the ground, and he wouldn't notice them unless he tripped over them. He was very absent-minded."

"That's a pretty good clue to go on. What did your brother look like, Miss Todd?"

"He was tall and rather thin. His hair was white and he was clean-shaven. His eyes and his teeth were very good. Even in spite of his age and all the reading and studying, he never had to wear glasses. Oh, yes—there's something else. He had an expression he often used, about as near swearing as he ever went. 'By jing!' it was. Whenever he was excited about anything or wanted to emphasize something he had said, he would always exclaim 'by jing!' I remember that he forgot himself in a lecture one day and said that. The dean spoke to him about it."

" 'By jing!' " remarked Frank thoughtfully. "It isn't an expression one hears every day."

"It was the only expression I can remember that was quite characteristic of Todham."

Miss Todd had little of further value to tell

them, and when the Hardy boys were by themselves later on they discussed the peculiarities of the missing professor.

"He forgets to tie his shoelaces and he says 'by jing!'" observed Joe. "It should be easy enough to pick him out with a description like that. It's strange he hasn't turned up long ago."

"Unless he met somebody who knew he was missing and who had heard of those little habits, he wouldn't be noticed. And it's just about a thousand chances to one that we would ever run across him."

"Well, we can at least make a note of it and tell Dad when he comes back. Chances are, he will never hear about those things, and Miss Todd may forget to tell him. It might help him a lot."

"I guess this is one mystery where we won't have much chance to help," said Frank ruefully. "Still, we'll do what we can."

But the Hardy boys were destined to take an even more active part in the mystery of Todham Todd than Fenton Hardy himself.

CHAPTER V

Plans for a Trip

Vacation time came, as it always does, although the days dragged, and when the last examination was written and the Hardy boys and their chums faced the long summer holidays, the boys had more exciting concerns than the affair of Todham Todd.

Miss Todd had left the Hardy home, after profuse thanks for the hospitality the family had shown her, and had returned to the college town. Mr. Hardy, after spending a day or so there, had gone on to parts unknown and it was assumed that he was following clues that he hoped would lead to the discovery of the missing professor.

"What are you going to do now?" asked Chet, on the first day of the holidays, when a number of the boys were sitting in the barn back of the Hardy home.

"Joe and I were figuring on a motorboat trip," said Frank.

34

"Good idea," Tony Prito remarked. "Where are you going?"

Frank shrugged.

"No place in particular. We hadn't come to that."

"As long as you go *somewhere,* it's all right with you, eh?" suggested Chet.

"That's about the size of it."

"I'd like to go on a motorboat trip myself," said Biff Hooper slowly. "As a matter of fact, I know of a place to go, but I don't know whether we can reach it in a boat."

"Where's that?"

"I was talking to an old sailor the other day in one of the villages down the shore and he was telling me a story about some caves that are said to be down on the main shore. We were talking about buried treasure, and that's how he brought the matter up. He said that there were old rumors of treasure in these caves."

"Treasure!" exclaimed Chet, brightening up. "That's our meat!"

"Of course, I'm not saying there *is* treasure in these caves. But the old chap said he had heard the story and he thought there might be something in it."

"In the caves, you mean," said the irrepressible Chet.

"Sure! These caves are out on the coast, south from the mouth of Barmet Bay."

"It wouldn't take us very long to go down and look the place over," Frank remarked.

"They're not easy to reach. I'm not sure that we can get to them by motorboat. But I believe there's a road runs down the coast in that neighborhood and we might be able to get there by land."

"We have the motorbikes," said Joe promptly.

"I'll find out more about it from the old chap and let you know," Biff promised.

"Find out more about the treasure," advised Chet. "Find out if it is in gold or silver and if we have to dig for it, and if there's enough to divide up among the crowd of us."

"So far as treasure is concerned, I don't hold much stock in these stories usually," said Biff. "But this old chap said that a gang of wreckers at one time lived in these caves. They had a pleasant little habit of changing the lights on the buoys along the reefs and wrecking ships. Then they would rob the vessels and store the loot in the caves."

"Good night!" exclaimed Tony. "Regular pirates."

"I'll say they were. Of course, all this was years ago. The gang was wiped out eventually and some of the leaders were hanged, but this old chap I was talking to said that very little of the loot was recovered. Of course, it may have been sold or shipped away, but he believes a lot of it is still hidden in the caves.''

"Hasn't any one ever hunted for it?"

"Oh, yes. But they've never found anything.''

"Why should we?" asked Chet.

"Why shouldn't we? And what does it matter if we don't? We might have some fun making the trip.''

"I think it's a good idea!" approved Frank Hardy. "We can take the motorcycles, run down there and poke around, and then come back. Of course I don't think we'll find any treasure, but it'll give us some sort of an objective, anyway.''

"Suits me,'' declared Chet. "My motorbike is hereby enlisted. I can take Biff along in the side car.''

"And we have our machines,'' Joe said. "Tony can ride with one of us.''

"We ought to have a mighty good trip,'' said Frank. "How long do you think we should be away, Biff?''

"It will take about a day and a half to reach that part of the coast, for the roads aren't very good, and then it will take another day or so finding these caves. If we want to do any exploring I guess we could stick around for

the rest of the summer and still have lots left
to do.''

"Well, we won't stay for the rest of the
summer. But about a week or ten days should
give us a good outing.''

"That suits me,'' said Chet. "I have other
things to do in the holidays besides crawling
around in caves.''

It was decided that the lads should inform
their parents of the projected trip and make
ready immediately. They planned to leave
Bayport in two days, as they wanted a day in
which to overhaul their motorcycles and get
everything in readiness. Tony Prito was dubious about getting permission, as his father
had been talking of putting him to work in the
wholesale fruit depot for a few weeks during
the summer season.

When the Hardy boys went into the house
to tell their mother about the trip to the caves,
they found that their father had just returned.
He was unpacking his bag as they entered the
hall.

"Hello, Dad!'' they greeted him. "What
luck?''

Fenton Hardy shook hands with his sons and
returned to the bag.

"What kind of luck do you mean?'' he asked.

"In the Todd case? Did you find the professor?''

"No," said the detective, "I didn't find the professor."

"Didn't you get any trace of him at all?"

"I found traces of him, all right. He's still alive, which is the main thing I learned."

"And yet you couldn't find him?" asked Joe.

"I followed him through half a dozen towns and cities, but I must say he is mighty elusive. He was always about three jumps ahead of me."

"He knew you were looking for him?"

"I don't think so. He wasn't running away from me. But he keeps on the move and he jumps around from one place to another without any rhyme or reason, so he was hard to follow. I finally lost track of him."

"That's tough," said Frank. "Where did you lose the trail?"

"At a little place called Claymore, about fifty miles south of here. He had been seen there last week, but he went away and no one knew where I could find him. So I gave up the search and came home."

"Have you dropped the case?"

Fenton Hardy laughed.

"Did you ever hear of me dropping a case before it was cleared up in one way or another?"

"No," admitted Frank. "But I thought you may have considered it a waste of time."

"It was a waste of time to keep following him about and never catching up with him. I decided to try another angle. Oh, we'll pick up Todham Todd yet."

"Joe and I have some information for you. But perhaps you know it already. Miss Todd gave us a few facts about her brother's appearance—"

"I have all that. I have a pretty good description of him, and I managed to get hold of a photograph at the college."

"Did you hear about his shoelaces?" asked Joe, excitedly.

"His shoelaces?"

"Miss Todd said her brother was mighty absent-minded and that quite often he forgot to tie up his shoelaces."

Mr. Hardy was interested.

"I didn't hear that one," he said. "It might be valuable. I'll make a note of it. A clue like that might mean a great deal in a case like this."

"And about 'by jing?' " asked Frank.

"By jing?"

"It's an expression he used. He never swears, but once in a while he says 'by jing!' if he is excited."

"That's something new, too. In all the information I picked up about Todham Todd I didn't hear anything about that expression or about the shoelaces, and they are two of the most important clues I could ask.''

The boys were gratified that they had gained this much information for their father's benefit. They knew that although Fenton Hardy had given up the direct search for the missing professor, he would never abandon the case until there was a definite solution one way or the other.

"Have you found why he disappeared from home?" asked Joe.

"I imagine he simply lost his memory," said Mr. Hardy. "At the present time, from what information I could pick up, he has no idea that his real name is Todham Todd. His memory is completely gone and he isn't able to remember anything of his past life. Probably if he met his sister again or some old acquaintance, it might all come back to him. He is wandering around, trying to find out who he is and where he comes from."

"Poor old chap!" said the boys sympathetically.

"He evidently had some money on his person when he disappeared, because he hasn't been in want, and the reason it was so hard to follow him was because he didn't stay in any one town more than a day or so. Just long enough to know that it wasn't his own town and that he could learn nothing about himself there. Then he would go on to the next place. But he'll turn up, I'm sure. I have a number of places being watched, where he's likely to put in an appearance some time, and I'll be notified at once.''

''In the meantime,'' promised Frank, ''we'll keep our eyes peeled for him. But we'll not be able to help much for a couple of weeks yet.''

''Why?''

''We're going on a motorbike jaunt down the coast to look over some caves.''

''Hidden treasure?'' asked their father, his eyes twinkling.

''Perhaps.''

''I hope you make a million,'' laughed Mr. Hardy. ''I'll try to find Todham Todd before you come back.''

CHAPTER VI

The Missing Motorcycle

"I wish I were a boy," sighed Callie Shaw.

Iola Morton looked up from her ice-cream soda.

"Me, too."

"It's tough luck that you're not," said Joe Hardy. "We'd like to have you along on the trip with us."

"Boys have all the luck. Girls have to stay at home."

The Hardy boys, Chet Morton, and Biff Hooper were celebrating their departure by treating Callie Shaw and Iola Morton—and incidentally, themselves—to ice-cream at the Bon Ton Confectionery Shop. Iola, a plump, dark girl, was Chet's sister, and fully as fun-loving as her brother. Of all the girls at Bayport High she was the special favorite of Joe, as Callie Shaw, brown-haired and brown-eyed, was above all other girls in Frank's opinion.

"This one is my treat," Joe announced. "Another soda won't hurt any one."

It was a warm afternoon and the others promptly accepted. Six tall, frosted glasses of soda, pink and white and orange in color were placed before them and imbibed with many gurgles of satisfaction.

"Well, sis," remarked Chet, "I don't know but that I'd trade places with you."

"Yes, you would!" said Iola ironically. "You wouldn't give up that trip for a million dollars."

"I've just been thinking that you're lucky to be staying in town. You'll be able to have ice-cream sodas and we shan't."

"That's true, too," said Joe reflectively. He was very fond of sodas, and he had not considered the matter in this light before.

"Yes, but think of all the fun you'll have. And if you find any treasure in those caves you'll be able to eat ice-cream sodas for the rest of your lives."

"Our lives wouldn't last very long if we did nothing but eat sodas after we came back," laughed Frank. "How about another?"

The girls shook their heads. Chet groaned.

"This is my fifth to-day," he said. "I *could* take another but I wouldn't have any room left for supper. Guess we'd better quit."

"We'd better," agreed Biff. "If you're sick to-morrow morning we'll start without you."

The thought of this possibility drove all desire for another ice-cream soda from Chet Morton's mind and the boys and girls left the Bon Ton. As they would not be seeing one another again before the start of the trip, Callie and Iola said good-bye to Biff and the Hardy boys.

"We'll miss you," Callie assured them. "The town won't seem the same without you."

"It won't be, either," grinned Chet. "It'll be a lot quieter when we clear out."

"Our house will be quieter, at any rate," Iola agreed. "It'll be a relief when you're gone, Chet."

"That's a sister for you! Frank, you and Joe are lucky. You have no sisters."

"I don't know about that," replied Frank. "If we had sisters like Callie and Iola we wouldn't have any kick."

Chet and his sister, in spite of all their good-natured banter, got along very well together. So, with much laughter and good wishes, the friends parted, and the Hardy boys went home to finish their packing.

Next morning found the four boys bowling along a country road leading out of Bayport, on the first stage of their journey to the caves on the coast. Greatly to their disappointment, Tony Prito had been unable to come with them, as his father needed him. Biff Hooper and Chet rode together. Frank and Joe, of course, had each his own motorcycle.

It was an ideal summer morning, cool and bright. The boys carried their blankets and cooking utensils, but they had agreed it would be best not to carry too many provisions, as food could be purchased along the way as it was needed.

"This won't be our first experience searching through caves," called out Frank, who was in the lead of the little procession.

"It will be old stuff to you chaps," answered Biff. "I sure wish I had been with you when you were going through the caves below the Shore Road."

He referred to the experience of the Hardy boys when they were in search of the automobiles that thieves had hidden in secret caves beneath the cliffs along the Shore Road above Barmet Bay.

"By the way," said Chet, "did you know that one of that gang of rascals escaped from jail the other day?"

This was news to the others. When the Hardy boys discovered the stolen cars they also aided in the round-up of the gang of automobile thieves, some of whom had been sentenced to long terms of imprisonment. Others, who had been merely tools of the ring-leaders of the outfit, were given lighter sentences in the local jail.

"Who was that?" asked Joe.

"Carl Schaum. He made a getaway the day before yesterday. The police were keeping quiet about it because they thought they might catch him again before the news leaked out But he's clear away."

"Carl Schaum!" exclaimed Frank. "He was one of the chaps who got off lightly."

"And to my mind he was one of the worst rascals of the lot," added Joe.

"Well, he's at large now. They haven't been able to trace him. He's a tough bird, all right."

"Carl Schaum used to live around here, didn't he?" asked Biff.

"Sure. He used to live just outside the city. He's been in and out of plenty of scrapes. A real bad egg."

"Oh, probably the police will pick him up again," Biff said. "He won't get very far. It's a cinch he won't hang around Bayport."

"Not if he knows what's good for him," remarked Frank.

The road the boys had taken went south and then east toward the coast, through a beautiful countryside. The boys had been on their way a little over two hours, but already they were hot and dusty. Just at that moment, Joe spied a flash of blue among the trees beyond an inviting shady lane.

"Looks like a lake down there," he said. "What say we investigate?"

"I'm game," said Chet. "Maybe we can have a swim."

As time was not pressing and the boys were traveling leisurely, in no hurry to reach the caves, they at once fell in with the suggestion. Frank headed down the lane and in a few minutes the lads were riding beneath shady trees down toward the banks of a small lake that lay calm and clear among the woods. There was a wide, sandy beach, and with whoops of delight the boys at once brought their motorcycles to a stop, parked them beneath the trees by the road, and raced gayly down through the grass.

It was one of the finest natural swimming places they had ever seen and the boys lost no time flinging off their clothes and splashing out into the cool water. For about half an hour they enjoyed themselves as only boys can, swimming and diving, until at last, refreshed, they came up onto the beach and donned their garments again.

Their motorcycles had been parked just out of sight of the beach, because the road ran past the lake, about a hundred yards distant. However, the boys had given little thought to the safety of the machines because the lake was in a secluded spot and there was no sign of human habitation near by.

"I'll race you back!" shouted Frank, as they began to dress.

There was a mad scramble for clothes. Chet adroitly hurled one of Biff's shoes into a thicket, thinking thereby to get a head start on his chum, but Joe sat on Chet's trousers as he drew on his own socks, and Chet hunted in vain for the essential garments, losing more time than Biff did. All this byplay took time, and Frank, in the meanwhile, was dressing hastily but calmly, and was ready before any of the others. With a yell of triumph, he darted up the grassy slope.

Joe was next. Shoelaces dragging, he set out in pursuit. Chet did not even bother to put on his shoes but hastened after, his shirt open, and hanging onto his trousers with one hand while he fastened his belt. Biff, plunging about in the bush in search of the missing shoe, was last.

"First up!" shouted Frank. Then the others heard him give a sudden exclamation of surprise.

"What's the matter?" called Joe.

He ran up in time to see Frank standing in the roadway, an expression of consternation on his face.

"The bikes!" he exclaimed. "There are only two here!"

"What?" yelled Joe.

"One of our bikes is missing! What do you know about that!"

As Chet and Joe hastened up they saw that he was right. Where three motorcycles had been parked beside the road, there were only two left.

Frank's motorcycle was gone!

CHAPTER VII

CARL SCHAUM

FRANK HARDY wasted no time.

The motorcycle had been stolen. There was no doubt of that. That it had been stolen within that past five minutes, he knew. When the boys were coming out of the water he thought he had heard the clatter of a machine, but at the time he had paid no attention to the sound, thinking it came from the main road.

"Come on!" he shouted. "We'll chase him."

"Which way has he gone?" gasped Chet.

Frank looked at the road. It was not a traveled thoroughfare and weeds and grass were in the ruts. It was impossible to see any sign of the tire tread.

"Joe and I will go ahead," he decided. "Chet, you and Biff go on back to the main road on your bike. If you don't get any trace of him, wait for us."

He sprang onto Joe's motorcycle and his brother leaped up behind. Biff Hooper was

51

just emerging from the bushes and Chet quickly told him what had happened.

In a moment the two machines were roaring off along the road in opposite directions, Chet and Biff returning to the highway and the Hardy boys going on down the country lane.

Once past the lake, Joe and Frank found the going was rough. Presumably, it was just a lane connecting with the highway, and there was little traffic over it. The motorcycle bumped along, Frank letting the machine out as much as he dared.

They came to a dusty spot in the lane and Frank gave a cry of exultation.

"This is the way he went! There's the tire marks!"

Clearly defined in the dust was the imprint of the tread. The boys knew they were on the right track, but they knew that the thief was undoubtedly proceeding as quickly as they were, if not faster.

Could they overtake him?

Coming to a more level stretch of road, Frank risked a greater speed and the motorcycle leaped forward in a cloud of dust. There were many curves and the high trees obscured a view of the road ahead so they had no idea how close they were to the fugitive.

Owing to the roar of their own machine they could not have heard the clatter of the other

motorcycle even if it had been only a short distance ahead. They could only trust to their
own speed and to the chance that the thief
had not obtained too much of a start.

Suddenly, as they swerved around a bend in
the road, Joe gave a cry of delight.

In the distance, on an open stretch, half-
hidden by a heavy cloud of dust, a motorcycle
was hurtling toward an expanse of paved highway that lay like a white ribbon far beyond the
trees.

"That's him!" Joe shouted.

But Frank had already seen the dark object
ahead.

He let the machine out to its fullest speed.
He knew that if the fugitive once gained the
highway it would be impossible to overtake
him. It was now or never.

But the country road was deceptive.

Just a few yards away, he spied a culvert.
It had been poorly constructed and a bad bump
was inevitable. It was suicidal to take it at
their present speed.

He desperately tried to slacken pace, but the
machine reached the rise in the road in a moment, lurched over it, seemed to leap through
the air, and then hit the road again with a
crash. There was a tremendous jolt.

Frank's grip was almost torn from the han-
dlebars, but he held on tightly. Joe had

grasped him tightly around the waist and still retained his seat.

The motorcycle swerved, skidded wildly, and headed toward the ditch.

But Frank had set himself for the shock of going over the culvert and he acted almost instinctively.

Had he been unprepared he would certainly have lost control of the motorcycle and both he and Joe might have been killed. He swung the hurtling machine back into mid-road again just when it seemed that it was about to crash into the deep ditch. He did not slacken speed, for that would have meant a dangerous skid.

By skillful handling, he settled the machine on the smoothest part of the road again and it roared on down the stretch.

The fugitive, too, seemed to be having trouble. The motorcycle ahead was lurching and bouncing in an alarming manner and its speed had slackened. Frank's experienced eye saw that the thief had encountered a rough and treacherous piece of road that ran for about half a mile before it met the main highway.

Suddenly they saw the machine swerve wildly and go completely over on its side. The driver was thrown into the middle of the road.

"He's done for!" Frank shouted.

But his joy was short-lived. The thief had

not given up yet. He scrambled to his feet and returned to the motorcycle, righted it, and leaped into the saddle. The machine, evidently undamaged, bounded forward again.

However, the accident had given the Hardy boys a chance to make up ground and they had gained considerably. In a few moments they reached the beginning of the rough section of the road and the fugitive was no more than two hundred yards ahead.

The two motorcycles lurched and bounded over the bumpy surface. Frank saw that the thief was not a first-class driver. He seemed to be having a great deal of trouble keeping the stolen machine on the road and did not dare travel at high speed.

As for himself, he saw that he would have to take chances. He shouted to Joe, "Hang on!" and let the motorcycle out as much as he dared.

It was a rough ride. More than once it seemed as though they would crash, but they steadily gained on the fugitive.

The man looked behind. He saw that he had no hope of reaching the highway.

The stolen motorcycle came to a stop. The rider leaped out into the road and ran toward the ditch. Beyond it there was a fence and a high bank of trees. Through the ditch and over the fence scrambled the fugitive. He looked back again just as the Hardy boys drew up beside the abandoned machine and then disappeared among the trees.

The boys were at first inclined to follow, and Joe dashed toward the ditch in pursuit. But Frank's better counsel prevailed.

"Let him go," he said. We'd never find him in that underbrush, and he might just double back to the road again and clear out on the motorcycle. We've got the machine back. That's the main thing."

Reluctantly, Joe came back.

"Yes, we've got the machine. But I'd like to lay my hands on that crook."

"Didn't you recognize him?"

Joe shook his head.

"I only caught a glimpse of his face but it seems to me I've seen him before."

"We've both seen him before."

"Where?"

"The Shore Road gang."

"The auto thieves?"

Frank nodded his head in assent.

"Then," exclaimed Joe, "that must be Carl Schaum! All the others are in jail."

"That's who it is, all right. I recognized him the moment he looked back."

"I wish I had chased him!" declared Joe.

"He's likely putting a lot of distance between himself and us just now. I guess the reason he stole the motorcycle was to help him in his getaway, for the police are looking for him since he escaped from jail.''

"If we had caught him we would have had to take him back to Bayport anyway,'' Joe remarked philosophically. "It would have interrupted our trip. Perhaps it's just as well.''

"He'll be picked up somewhere else. I'm glad he didn't get my motorcycle. That would have upset the trip even worse.''

Frank examined the machine. It had been slightly damaged by the upset on the rough road and there were a few dents and scrapes, but there was nothing seriously wrong with it. He mounted the motorcycle and its staccato roar soon filled the air.

"Running as good as ever,'' he said, with satisfaction.

"Good! Shall we go back now?''

"We may as well. There's no use chasing Carl Schaum, and the others will be wondering what has happened.''

The brothers rode back toward the swimming pool and then out to the highway, where they found Chet and Biff waiting for them. Not having found any trace of the machine on the highway the chums had waited according to instructions. When they saw the brothers coming in view, each on his own machine, they raised a cheer.

"Good work!" shouted Chet. "Did you have to battle for it?"

"No battle at all," returned Frank, bringing the motorcycle to a stop. "An old friend of ours had just borrowed it for a little ride."

Chet looked at him incredulously. Frank laughed at the expression on his chum's face.

"An old friend!" exclaimed Biff. "I didn't know you had any friends around this part of the country."

"He wasn't exactly a friend. An acquaintance, I should say. Carl Schaum swiped the machine."

Chet and Biff whistled simultaneously.

"Schaum was the thief!" Biff exclaimed. "Are you sure?"

"Where is he?" demanded Chet. "Did you tie him up?"

"We didn't catch him," confessed Joe. "He left the bike in the road when he saw we were gaining on him. Then he cleared out over the fence and into the woods."

"That was too bad!" exclaimed Chet.

"Are you sure it was Carl Schaum?" asked Biff Hooper, for the second time.

"I got a good look at him," Frank said. "It was Carl Schaum, all right. When we get to the next town we'll tell the police. If they know he's around here at all they'll probably land him without much trouble."

Chet went over to his motorcycle.

"Well, the sooner we get to the next town, the better. We've lost quite a bit of time already. What say we start on again?"

The chums agreed that the discovery of the swimming hole had cost them considerably more time than they had expected, so accordingly they mounted their machines again and set out on the highway once more.

CHAPTER VIII

STRANGE DOINGS

THE Hardy boys and their chums spent the night at a hotel in a small village. They were up bright and early next morning, eager to reach the end of their journey. Had it not been for the delay consequent on the attempted theft of Frank's motorcycle, they might have reached the neighborhood of the caves that evening, but, as it was, they had a two hours' trip before them when they set out shortly after six o'clock.

Their immediate destination was a fishing village by the name of Glencove. It was a sleepy little place, quite picturesque but redolent of fishy odors, a typical hamlet of the kind. The boys were aware that Glencove was some distance north of the caves, but as they did not know the precise location of the "Honeycomb Cliffs," as they were called, they preferred to stop off at the village and get what information they could.

The general store, a ramshackle building

where one could buy anything from safety pins
to grindstones, where one could mail a letter,
put through a telephone call, or obtain garage
service, appeared to be the most likely spot.
Parking their machines by the wooden side-
walk, the lads went into the store, where they
found a venerable man with white whiskers
patiently scrutinizing his newspaper.

"I guess we'd better stock up on a few supplies, eh, fellows?" Frank suggested.

This had been their plan. Instead of bur-
dening their machines with provisions all the
way from Bayport, they had decided to get
supplies at the village nearest to the caves.

"Perhaps we won't have to stock up very
heavily," said Joe. "If the caves aren't far
away we may be able to drive up here when we
run short of grub."

"That," said the hungry Chet, "would be
terrible."

Frank turned to the old gentleman, who had
put aside his paper and was regarding them
through his thick-lensed spectacles with grave
curiosity, as though they were some new speci-
men of humanity entirely.

"How far is it to the place they call Honeycomb Cliffs?" he asked.

The old gentleman's eyes widened.

"Honeycomb Cliffs!" he said, in a high,
cracked voice. "Be ye goin' to pass by there?"

"We want to camp around there for a few days and we were figuring on buying some supplies. If it's far away we'll buy all we need right now and carry the stuff with us."

The old man leaned farther over the counter.

"Ye're agoin' to *camp* at Honeycomb Cliffs!" he exclaimed incredulously.

"Why, yes."

"For three or four days!"

"Perhaps longer."

The old gentleman shook his head solemnly.

"Ye're strange to these parts, ain't ye?"

"This is the first time we've ever been down this way."

"I thought so," returned the old man with a great air of satisfaction, as though his judgment had been verified.

"Well," said Frank, becoming a trifle impatient, "we'd still like to know how much farther we have to go."

"It's a matter of about ten mile by the road. Then ye'll have to walk a ways."

"Ten miles. Why, that isn't very far. We'll just buy enough food to last us a day or so and then if we need more one of us can come back here. There's no use packing along too much."

"And ye say ye're goin' to camp there?" persisted the old man, as though he could not quite grasp the fact.

"Yes. What's wrong about that? Aren't there any places we can pitch a tent?"

"Oh, yes, there's places ye can pitch a tent and I've no doubt but there's fishermen's cottages that you could find a room at. But if I was you I wouldn't do no campin' near Honeycomb Cliffs. That is," said the old man, "unless ye stay away from the caves."

"Why, that's what we came for," put in Biff. "We intend to explore the caves!"

The old man gave a perceptible gasp at this.

"Explore 'em! Lads, ye're crazy."

The old gentleman's attitude puzzled the boys extremely.

"Is it against the law?" Chet inquired.

"No, it ain't agin the law, but it's agin common sense."

"Why?"

"It just is—that's all," retorted the storekeeper, as though that explained everything.

"You don't mean to say it's dangerous!"

"Maybe. Maybe," returned their informant mysteriously. "It may not be dangerous, but it would be foolish. If ye'll take my advice ye'll stay away from them caves."

"Why?"

"There's some queer things been goin' on down there lately. Folks tell me the fishermen down that way are scared nigh to death."

"What are they afraid of?" asked Biff.

The old man shrugged eloquently.

"That's just it. Nobody knows. But there's been queer lights seen down around them caves. And shootin'."

"Shooting!"

"Guns goin' off," explained the storekeeper, as if they had failed to understand the word. "Mighty queer doin's, they say. Two men a'ready that tried to find out what was goin' on—they got shot at."

Chet whistled softly.

"This sounds good," he observed. "We may stay longer than we had intended."

"Ye may stay forever," growled the old man gloomily.

Frank smiled at this thrust.

"Has anybody any idea what's wrong?" he asked.

The storekeeper leaned across the counter and lowered his voice, in the manner of one imparting a deep secret.

"They do say," he declared, "that there's smugglin' of liquor in them parts."

"I suppose that's only natural. There's a lot of it along the coast, and the caves would make that an ideal spot."

"Well, whether there is or there ain't, the caves ain't healthy for strangers. If I was you lads, I'd stay away from there."

"Well, we've planned this trip and I think

we'll go through with it," Frank said. "If you'll fix us up with some supplies, we'll be on our way. We're not afraid of bootleggers."

"Do as ye like," the old man returned, as though washing his hands of any further responsibility. "But I'm warnin' ye. It ain't no place if ye're lookin' for a quiet outing."

"The one thing we're afraid of, is a *quiet* outing," Joe assured him. "Excitement," he added slangily, "is our meat."

"Ye'll get lots of it if ye go pokin' around them caves," the old gentleman predicted. "Mebbe a lot more than ye bargain for."

However, he was prevailed upon to sell the lads a quantity of provisions for their trip, although he accompanied the transaction by a running fire of dismal comments on the unlikelihood that they would ever be seen alive again. When he saw that they were determined to go to the caves, in spite of his admonitions, he wagged his head sadly and mumbled a few caustic remarks on the stubborness of boys in general who would never listen to their elders.

The Hardy boys and their chums, far from being frightened at the prospect of danger at Honeycomb Cliffs, were elated. They were disposed to disregard much of what the old man had said—the perils were most probably exaggerated in the re-telling—but there was no mistaking the old man's sincerity and they knew that undoubtedly there was a mystery of some kind concerning the neighborhood of the caves.

"What that mystery is, we're going to find out," said Joe, as they mounted their motorcycles again, duly laden with supplies. He expressed the determination of all.

"It looks a lot brighter," Chet agreed. "There's a chance of a bit of excitement now."

"Oh, probably there's nothing to it," scoffed Biff. "Somebody has seen a tramp's campfire on the cliffs and heard some one shooting at a rabbit, and started a big yarn out of it."

"Well, we are going to have our own fun exploring those caves, and if there's a mystery on foot, so much the better," said Joe.

The boys followed the directions given them by the old storekeeper and in due time left the coast road and turned down a rutty, torturous lane that ended on the open seashore, near a fisherman's cottage. The little house was built at the base of a hill and the beach ended at this point in towering cliffs. The lads could see a faint, winding path leading up the side of the hill back of the cottage.

"I know what they call this place," said Chet gravely.

"I don't think it has a name," said Biff.

"Oh, yes, they call this place Fish-hook."

"Fish-hook? Why?" asked Biff, neatly falling into the trap.

"Because it's at the end of the line."

With that, Chet brought his motorcycle to a stop. The Hardy boys also stopped, joining Chet in his laughter at the foolish look on Biff's face when he saw how he had been duped.

The storekeeper had told them that the fisherman's cottage was the last human habitation on the way to the caves and that they could very likely get permission to leave their machines there for safe-keeping. To reach the caves they had to climb the path up the hillside until they reached the top of the cliffs, then proceed for a considerable distance until they came to a deep ravine, where they could descend to the shore. They would then find themselves on a beach whereby they could reach the caves to right and to left. The cliffs themselves cut off access to the caves by any other route than the ravines, several of which were to be encountered in the three miles of steep coast, as at the northern and southern extremities the cliffs were sheer to the deep water and could not be skirted even at low tide.

The boys had scarcely dismounted from their motorcycles when the door of the cottage opened and a stocky, leathern-faced man of middle age emerged. He was plainly a fisherman and he came over to them, a look of surprise on his broad, good-natured countenance.

"What can I do for you, my lads?" he inquired. "It ain't often I see strangers here."

"We want to know if we could leave our motorcycles here for safe-keeping?" asked Frank.

"Certainly. Most certainly, you can. There's a shed back of the house, where you can put 'em. Is it just for an hour or so? Goin' up on the cliffs?"

"Perhaps for a few days. We were planning to go exploring among the caves."

The fisherman's expression changed instantly.

"Explorin' the caves!" he exclaimed. "You'd best go back home. There's strange doin's in the caves these days. It's no place for boys."

CHAPTER IX

The Storm

Chet Morton laughed.

"We heard there were some queer things happening around here, but that doesn't frighten us."

"There's nothing to laugh at, young man," returned the fisherman tartly. "I've lived here for twenty years and I'm no fool. The caves ain't healthy just now."

"Rum-runners, I suppose," said Frank.

But the fisherman scorned this suggestion.

"If it's rum-runners, they'd be bringin' their cargoes out to the road, wouldn't they? Not much sense in 'em hidin' the liquor in the caves and leavin' it there, is there?"

"I wouldn't think so. But perhaps they bring it out to the road quietly."

"Nothin' of the sort. It's been investigated. There's been no queer doin's on the road at all. All the queer doin's are right in the caves. If it was rum-runners, they'd be bringin' the stuff in by boat, and there ain't been any boats

69

seen around here that can't be accounted for.''

''Just what are the queer doings?''

''Lights, mostly. And shootin'.''

''But has no person been seen?''

''Not a livin' soul.''

''That's strange.''

''Strange ain't the word for it!'' declared the fisherman. ''It's downright spooky. Like ghosts or somethin'.''

''Do you believe in ghosts?'' asked Joe.

''I don't. If I did believe in ghosts, though, I'd say there was ghosts down in them caves lately and that's all I'd think about it. But not believin' in ghosts, I don't know what to think.''

''Have you gone down to the caves yourself?''

''I went down there a couple of weeks ago, but I didn't see anything until just when I was comin' back that night. Then I saw a light away down in one of the caves I'd been in just a couple of hours before. Next I heard two or three shots, and then a yell.''

''A yell!''

''The most awful screech I ever heard.''

''Well, that proves that there's *somebody* down there,'' remarked Biff.

''Maybe it does and maybe it don't. I wouldn't say it was a human voice I heard. More like an animal.''

"But an animal couldn't make a light."

"And there ain't many human bein's could make that yell. So there you are."

"Yells or no yells, we're going to explore the caves," declared Frank, with finality. "What say, fellows?"

"I'll tell the world we are!" exclaimed Chet. "You couldn't drive me away now with a squad of marines."

The fisherman shrugged.

"It's your funeral," he said. "I'm thinkin' you'll come away from there a lot faster than you go in."

"Perhaps," agreed Joe, with a grin. "And perhaps we'll find out just who or what is causing all the disturbance. We'll go prepared for anything that may happen to turn up, at any rate."

"You'll need to," said the fisherman gloomily. "Don't say that I didn't warn you. You're welcome to put your machines in the shed, and if you'd like a bite to eat, I guess my wife can fix up a bit of a snack for you."

This hospitality was appreciated by the boys and they saw that the fisherman's bark was worse than his bite, as the saying is, but they politely declined, as they had eaten just a short time before. Chet, who could—and would—eat at any time, was not very emphatic in his refusal; he would willingly have accepted the invitation. But the other lads were anxious to be going on.

"It's very good of you," said Frank, "and I hope you don't think we're rude in going ahead to the caves after your warning. But there are four of us, you see, and we think we can look after ourselves pretty well. So, if you'll just let us leave the motorcycles in the shed while we're around here we won't bother you any further."

"You're welcome to do that. And I suppose if you're bound to go on to the caves, nothin' I can say will stop you."

The fisherman led the way to the shed, where the motorcycles were safely stored. The machines would be under cover in the event of rain, and there was a stout padlock on the door that ensured their safety against being stolen. The lads unloaded their supplies and each filled his pack with provisions.

"Have we got everything?" asked Frank finally. "Matches, flashlights, revolver, bullets, bread, salt, coffee—"

"Everything needed for an expedition to the South Pole," said Chet, shifting his pack to a more comfortable position on his shoulders.

A complete check-up showed that they had everything they needed; so, after bidding good-bye to the fisherman, who drew them a rough map showing the route they should follow in order to reach the caves, they set out up the path just back of the cottage.

"Nobody seems very encouraging about this trip," said Biff, as they ascended the hillside.

"What do you think *can* be the trouble down in the caves?" asked Joe.

"Rum-runners, I'll bet! In spite of what the fisherman says, I can't think of any other explanation," Frank replied. "They probably have some way of getting the stuff out to the road without being seen. Underground passages, or something of the sort."

"It seems likely. The shots and the yells were just to frighten people away."

"Well, we should soon find out."

Although the hillside path had not seemed very formidable from the shore, the boys found that it was steeper than it looked, and it was more than an hour before they finally reached the top of the cliffs. Here a magnificent view awaited them. Far below, the fisherman's cottage seemed to lie at their very feet, like a toy house. The ocean lay like a flat blue floor, far to the east, north, and south, and back of them was a great, barren expanse of tumbled rock, without sign of path or road. Venturing close to the edge of the cliff, the lads saw a sheer wall of rock, many feet in height, at the bottom of which the waves were lapping.

"No wonder we couldn't reach the caves by skirting the shore!" said Frank. "The only way along the base of that cliff is by boat."

"We'll have to go ahead and search for the ravine the fisherman told us about," suggested Joe.

Chet looked up at the sky.

"Yes, and we can't afford to lose any time about it either. We're in for a storm."

Although the lads had noticed that the sun had gone behind a cloud, they had not seen the heavy black cloud banks massing above them, so intent had they been on their climb up the steep, winding path. Now, when they looked up, they saw that a storm was indeed imminent. The breeze bore to their ears a rumble of distant thunder.

"It looks like a bad one," said Biff. "We'd better hurry."

Without further ado, the boys hastened off along the faint trail that led among the rocks. They could see no sign of the ravine, but judged that it would be almost invisible until they came almost on it. Their progress was slow, as it was difficult to make haste over the rocks and boulders.

The storm came up swiftly. Within ten minutes the clouds were banked blackly in the sky above. A streak of livid lightning rent the gloom and there was a peal of thunder.

"We're out of luck if we can't find shelter before this storm breaks," panted Chet. The air was insufferably close. A few scattered raindrops warned the lads that they had no time to lose.

They plodded on, mentally wishing that they had remained at the fisherman's cottage but realizing that it was too late to turn back now.

Another flash of lightning, a terrific thunderclap, and the storm broke.

Rain began falling heavily. It streamed down from the black skies as though the clouds had opened. The wind rose. Far below them the surf boomed and the waves crashed against the base of the cliff. Rain poured in a veritable deluge. The lads had neglected to provide themselves with slickers, as they were already burdened by the weight of their supplies, and they were soon drenched to the skin.

They stumbled on, scarcely able to follow the faint path in the gloom. Lightning flickered, thunder crashed constantly, the wind rose to a howl. There was not the slightest vestige of shelter, not even a tree, out on this rocky waste. Frank looked in vain for a boulder large enough to offer some protection.

They plunged forward into a streaming wall of rain.

Frank was in the lead. Chet and Biff were next, and Joe brought up the rear. They could scarcely see one another in the gathering gloom. On and on they went, heads bent to the storm, and, to Chet especially, time seemed to stand still in a gray world.

Suddenly Frank looked behind, then came to a stop.

"Where is Joe?" he shouted, above the clamor of the gale.

The others looked back.

Joe had vanished.

CHAPTER X

The Cave

THE boys gazed at one another in surprise.

"Where on earth did Joe disappear to?" exclaimed Biff Hooper.

They peered into the gray oblivion of the storm, but the rain was teeming down in such heavy torrents and the gloom was so intense that it was impossible to see more than twenty yards away.

"We'll have to go back," decided Frank quickly. "He probably sat down to rest and got lost when he tried to catch up with us again."

They retraced their steps over the rocks, keeping close together. They shouted again and again, but in the roar of wind, rain, and thunder they knew there was little chance that Joe would hear them.

"I never thought to look back," said Chet. "I thought he was right behind us."

"Same here," declared Biff. "He might have dropped back five or ten minutes ago and we didn't know it."

The search seemed hopeless. It was late in the afternoon and already getting dark. Once in a while they stopped and listened, hoping to hear some faint cry from Joe, but there was nothing.

"Perhaps he fell down and hurt himself," suggested Frank. "He may be lying behind some of these big rocks and we can't see him."

The boys searched patiently.

Joe Hardy was nowhere to be found.

They did not dare scatter, for fear of losing one another, but they hunted among the rocks, realizing the hopeless nature of their quest. At last they halted, standing in a little group, with rain pouring down on them.

Frank expressed the fear they had all held for the past few minutes.

"I wonder if he could have fallen over the cliff!"

They had been going along within a few yards of the uneven edge of the cliff and they realized that, in the rain and the dim light, it would have been easy for Joe to have stumbled into the abyss. They turned sick at the thought of the frightful plunge, ending in certain death, had he tumbled over the verge.

Suddenly, above the roar of the storm, they heard a faint cry.

"Listen!" cried Frank.

Breathlessly, they waited.

Again came the cry.

"Help! Help!"

It was from almost at their feet.

Frank ran quickly forward. At the very edge of the cliff, he stopped and peered down.

Over to one side, a few feet below the top of the sheer wall of rock, he spied a dark figure.

It was Joe!

He seemed to be clinging directly to the side of the cliff.

Hastily shouting to the others, Frank ran across the rocks until he came to a place immediately above where he had seen his brother. He flung himself flat and peered over into the dizzy depths.

Just beneath, he could see Joe's white face. His brother was clinging to a small bush growing out of the side of the cliff. Had the bush been his only support, he would not have been able to maintain his hold, but fortunately there was a ledge of rock, a few inches wide, in which he had managed to implant his feet. Thus he had clung to the face of the cliff.

"Quick!" shouted Frank, to the others. He realized the need for haste. "He's here!"

"I can't hold on much longer!" called Joe, in a strained voice.

"We'll get you out of this," Frank assured him. But his heart sank when he saw that Joe was beyond his reach.

Biff and Chet came running up, and Frank tersely explained the situation to them.

"There's only one thing to do," he said. "Both of you hang on to me while I lower myself over."

Biff peeped over the edge of the cliff.

"You'll never make it," he said. "You'll both be killed."

"We're not going to stand idle until he gets exhausted and lets go his hold," declared Frank. "It's the only chance, and I'm going to take it."

He flung himself down and began to edge forward until he was leaning far over the verge. Biff and Chet seized his ankles and set themselves by digging their heels against the rocks. Bit by bit, Frank lowered himself, headfirst, over the side. His outstretched hands were but a few inches away from Joe's wrists. Joe still clung to the bush that had saved his life.

Frank dared not look down, for he was hanging at a dizzy height. He closed his eyes.

"A little more," he called out.

He swung lower and gripped Joe's wrists. He secured a tight hold. There was no time to lose, as he knew it would take every ounce of strength he possessed to drag his brother back to safety, and he was growing weaker all the time.

"Ready, Joe?"

"All right," gasped Joe.

"Haul away!"

Chet and Biff began dragging Frank back. There was a double weight now, for Joe relaxed his grip on the root to which he had been clinging and was now dangling in space, supported only by Frank's firm grip on his wrists. Frank had no idea that his brother weighed so much; the strain was terrific.

Gradually, however, he was drawn back to safety. For one horrible moment he thought he was losing his hold on Joe's wrists, as their locked hands reached the edge of the precipice. But Chet, leaning forward, seized the back of Joe's shirt, clung to him while Biff scrambled over, and together they hauled him up onto the rocks.

For a moment, neither of the Hardy boys could say a word, they were so exhausted by the ordeal. Above them the storm still raged, the rain still poured from the black skies, the lightning still flickered, and the thunder still boomed and rumbled.

"Boy, that was a narrow squeak!" said Chet solemnly, at last.

"Don't talk about it," said Joe, closing his eyes, as though to shut out the memory of the sight. "I can still see the waves away down beneath me. I was never so near death in my life."

"We'll stick closer together after this. How did it happen?" Frank asked.

"I stopped to tie my shoelace. When I looked up again I couldn't see you chaps at all, so I began to run to catch up. I didn't realize I was so near the edge of the cliff. Then some of the rock must have broken off under my feet, because everything gave way and I felt myself falling."

"You're mighty lucky you're here to tell us about it," said Biff.

"I'll say I am! I just managed to grab that root growing out of the side of the cliff and I hung there until I thought my arms would be pulled out of their sockets. I thought I'd never be able to hold on until you found me."

"It was quite a while before we missed you."

"At any rate, I *couldn't* have held on, but I managed to find that ledge and got my feet on it. That rested me. I was certainly glad when I heard you fellows shouting for me."

Recovering somewhat from their grueling experience, Frank and Joe Hardy got to their feet.

"Let's run for it," suggested Chet. "We're drenched to the skin, as it is, but I don't want to stay out in this storm any longer than I have to."

With one accord, the boys resumed their journey over the rocks. This time no one lagged

behind. For safety's sake they stayed close together and well away from the verge of the
cliff.

In a short time Frank gave a cry of delight.
"The ravine!" he yelled.

Through the pouring rain, just a few yards
ahead, they discerned a deep cut in the rocks.

They scrambled toward it. The ravine was
deep and the slope was steep, but they had been
fortunate in reaching it just at a point where
a path led down among the rocks.

Far below, they could see the beach and the
breaking rollers.

Slipping and stumbling, the boys made their
way down the steep, winding path in the downpour. The storm was unabated. Its violence,
on the contrary, seemed to have increased. The
rain came down in sheets.

Halfway down the path, Joe gave a cry of
excitement.

"A cave!"

He pointed down toward the base of the cliff,
just visible from the path.

There, but a short distance from the breaking
waves, was a dark hole in the steep wall of rock.

CHAPTER XI

FOOTSTEPS IN THE NIGHT

WITH the goal in sight, the Hardy boys and their chums hastened down the treacherous path, along the steep side of the ravine. The path was slippery and little rivulets of water ran at their feet. Chet Morton slipped and went sprawling in the mud, getting to his feet with exclamations of disgust.

"Oh, well," he said philosophically, "I can't be any wetter than I am already."

Frank consoled him.

"When we get to that cave we'll light a fire and dry ourselves out a bit."

They at length reached the floor of the ravine where little streams of water were coursing from the upper levels to the sea and splashing across to the beach. It was only a few yards from there to the black entrance of the cave, which was well above the reach of high tide.

Frank led the way.

He took a flashlight from his pack as the boys

hastened into the dark mouth of the cavern. They were in shelter, at any rate, and they could look out at the streaming rain and feel thankful that they had a roof over their heads, although that roof was a rocky one.

Frank directed the beam of the flashlight into the gloomy interior and in its gleam he saw that their shelter was no mere niche in the face of the cliff, but a cave that led to dark and unknown depths.

"Looks as if we can start our exploring right here and now," he said.

"Explore my neck!" grumbled Chet. "Let's have a fire."

"How about firewood?" inquired the practical Biff.

This had not occurred to the others. They glanced at one another in dismay.

"That's right too," said Joe. "There's not much wood around these rocks and it's all wet by now, anyway."

"Nothing but driftwood," Frank observed disconsolately. "The rain has drenched it." He glanced out, and along the shore he spied a few bits of wood tossed up by the waves, but they were sodden and useless.

"This is going to be fine," said Chet. "We'll have to shiver here all night without a fire. A great beginning to our visit!"

To tell the truth, the boys were feeling none

too cheerful over the prospect, for they were all cold, wet, and hungry and they had been looking forward to dry clothes and a hot meal by a roaring fire. Now it seemed that they were doomed to spend the night in the cheerless shelter of a damp, cold cave, without the vestige of a blaze.

"Thank goodness our blankets are dry, at any rate," Joe said philosophically.

Frank moved farther back into the cave, with the flashlight illuminating the way. Suddenly he gave an exclamation of mingled astonishment and delight.

"Well! can you beat this, fellows?"

"What have you found?"

"Firewood."

"Where?"

The others came hastening over to Frank Hardy.

"Look!" Frank cast the beam of the flashlight against the black wall near by.

Full in the center of the circle of radiance, they saw a neat pile of wood. It had not been placed there by accident; that much was certain. It had been stacked carefully by human hands.

Frank stepped over and picked up one of the sticks.

"Good dry driftwood. We don't have to worry about a fire now."

"I wonder who on earth piled it in here?" remarked Biff.

Chet shrugged.

"Why worry about that? The main thing is that some thoughtful soul has been kind enough to put it here, and we're the boys who are going to use it. Where shall we light the fire, Frank?"

"Right here, I guess. This is far enough back from the entrance so that we won't have to worry about the rain beating in. It's certainly queer how that wood comes to be here, though."

"Probably the mysterious chaps who are doing all the yelling and shooting," said Biff. "We'll be out of luck if this is *their* cave we've stumbled on."

"It's ours now. I don't see any 'No Trespassing' signs." Frank began carrying wood over to the center of the cave. Then he set down the flashlight, took out his pocketknife, and whittled at a particularly dry stick until he had a small heap of shavings. Carefully stacking a few of the smaller sticks over the shavings and the larger sticks above, crosswise so that there were plenty of air spaces, he took a match from his waterproof case and ignited it, putting it to the shavings. They flared up brightly.

Anxiously, the boys watched the little blaze.

The flames caught the small sticks, which snapped and crackled. Then, as the fire rose higher, the heavier wood was ignited, and in a short time the boys had a roaring fire. Never had a campfire been so welcome. Frank had been afraid that lack of a draught in the cave might cause so much smoke that they would be almost smothered, but evidently there was some opening in the roof, some overhead passage that acted in the nature of a chimney, for the smoke was carried off above.

As the warmth of the fire penetrated the cave, the boys took off their drenched clothes and spread them about the blaze, in the meantime wrapping themselves in the heavy blankets they had brought with them. Chet produced the frying pan, and the fragrant odor of sizzling bacon soon permeated their refuge. He improvised a tripod from which was suspended a tin pail, duly filled with rain water that coursed in a gushing stream just beside the mouth of the cave, and in a short time the coffee was boiling.

The boys never enjoyed a meal more than they enjoyed their supper in the cave. The driftwood blazed and crackled, casting a cheerful glow, illuminating the rocky ceiling and walls of the underground chamber. With crisp bacon, bread toasted brown before the fire, hot coffee and jam. they ate ravenously, and at last sat back with deep sighs of sheer content.

"This old cave isn't so bad after all," said Chet, wrapping his blanket around him like a cocoon and wriggling his toes toward the flames.

The others glanced toward the entrance of the cavern.

It was pitch dark outside, and still raining. They could hear the constant beat of the downpour, the incessant roar of the surf, the splash of the waves, the moaning of the cold wind out in the blackness of the night, and the cave seemed the most comfortable place in the world.

"We owe a vote of thanks to the chap who stacked this driftwood in here," said Biff.

"I'll tell the world!" declared Joe. "We'd have been shivering and hungry yet if it hadn't been for him."

"I wonder who he could have been," mused Frank.

"Perhaps somebody who was down here searching for the smugglers or bootleggers or whoever has been raising all the fuss around here," his brother suggested.

"He hasn't shown up yet," Chet remarked cheerfully. He looked out into the storm and shivered. "Somehow, I have an idea he won't be along to-night, either," he added, edging nearer the fire.

"I guess we'd better have a good night's

sleep and then start our exploring to-morrow,"
Frank said. "We can start right on this cave,
for that matter. It seems to lead back for quite
a distance."

"Sleep sounds good to me." Biff yawned.

Although part of the floor of the cave was
rocky, much of it was sand, which provided a
fairly comfortable resting place. The boys
were tired after their long journey, so they
wrapped themselves up in their blankets and
were soon drowsily chatting, while the fire died
lower and lower.

At last only the embers glowed crimson in the
darkness. Chet Morton was already snoring.
Soon, all were asleep.

The fire was a scarlet eye in the blackness of
the cave. Beyond the entrance, rain still
poured in a seemingly endless torrent and the
surf roared dully.

An hour passed. Two hours.

Joe, who had been sleeping soundly, was
awakened. At first he did not realize where he
was, could not imagine why he was sleeping on
the ground, wrapped in a heavy blanket, and
then it gradually came back to him and he re-
membered about the cave.

He was just about to turn over and go to
sleep again, wondering vaguely what had
aroused him, when he heard a footstep.

It came from close by.

He listened, and then he heard it again. Some one was moving cautiously about in the darkness.

Joe raised himself on one elbow and peered into the gloom. But he could see nothing. However, he reasoned that it was probably only one of his chums.

When he heard a rustle, he spoke.

"Is that you, Frank?"

The words rang out clearly in the silence of the cave.

But the consequence was surprising. Instead of the reassuring voice of his brother, Joe heard a muffled exclamation, quick footsteps as some one ran across the floor of the cave, and then the 'rash of a fallen rock.

CHAPTER XII

A Disappearance

"Who is that?" demanded Joe Hardy, scrambling to his feet.

There was no answer. He heard the sound of running footsteps gradually growing fainter.

"Hey, there!" he shouted, now thoroughly aroused. "Fellows! Wake up!"

He stumbled about in the darkness, trying to find his flashlight and his chums. Then he heard Chet's sleepy voice:

"What's the matter? It isn't morning yet. Lemme sleep."

"Wake up! There's some one prowling around here."

"What's that?" called out Frank, from the darkness.

"There was some one else in the cave just now. He woke me up."

"Perhaps it was only Biff. Hey, Biff!"

A deep sigh. Then Biff mumbled:

"Whaddaya want?"

"Wake up." Frank switched on his flashlight and he turned it on each member of the startled group. "Everybody here?"

"Sure!" replied Biff, sitting up in his blanket. "What's wrong?"

"Joe says somebody was prowling around the cave."

"It wasn't me. I've been sleeping like a log."

"It wasn't me either," spoke up Chet.

"I guess I was right, then," declared Joe. "There really *was* somebody. I thought for a minute it might be one of you playing a trick on the rest of us."

"We're all accounted for," said Frank. He got up and tossed a stick of wood on the embers of the fire. In a few minutes it began flaming up brightly, casting a circle of illumination through the cave. "Tell us about it, Joe."

Joe thereupon told of hearing the mysterious footsteps in the cave, of calling out and of hearing the exclamation, the crash of the rock, and the running footsteps as the intruder fled.

"Did he go out the front way?"

Joe shook his head.

"No. He seemed to go farther into the cave, toward the back."

"Well, then," said Frank decisively, "we'll just go and look for him. If he went that way, he's in the cave yet."

"Aw, let's look for him in the morning," protested Chet, as he rubbed his eyes. "I think Joe was dreaming."

"It was no dream. I *heard* him walking around. It wasn't any of us, so it must have been a burglar—or somebody."

"What would a burglar come around here for?"

"Perhaps it's the chap who piled up all that wood," said Frank. "Maybe this is his cave and when he came in and heard Joe call out he got frightened and ran."

"That sounds more reasonable. Anyway, we'll take a look around for him. He can't be far away."

The boys hurriedly dressed. They were soon wide awake, excitement having banished all desire for further sleep.

"We were going to explore in here, anyway," said Frank, as he took his flashlight and led the way toward the back of the cave.

The boys confronted an arch in the rock, an opening that seemed to lead into a tunnel. They approached it cautiously, and Frank often turned the light on the floor to make sure that no pitfalls lay before them.

Frank went into the tunnel first. In single file, the others followed.

It was about fifteen feet in length and about six feet high. As the floor was of solid rock, they were unable to find any foot-prints that would serve to prove that the intruder had passed that way.

The tunnel led to another cave.

"Why, there's a regular chain of caves in here!" exclaimed Joe, as the boys stepped out into a massive underground chamber.

"Our cave was only the beginning," said Chet.

In the glow of their flashlights they saw that the cave in which they now stood had a number of dark openings in the walls. These were, presumably, tunnels leading into further caves beyond.

"There are a dozen different passages out of here. Our friend might have taken any of them," said Frank.

"We'll tackle the biggest," suggested Biff.

"Good idea. If we don't get anywhere, we'll try the others."

The largest tunnel was immediately ahead. Frank, accordingly, stepped into the gloomy passage. The others followed.

"When I was going to sleep to-night, I never thought I'd wake up and take part in an exploring trip underground before morning," observed Chet.

Frank gave an exclamation.

"Here's what we were looking for!" he cried.

"What?"

"A footprint."

The others crowded around him.

Clearly discernible in the radiance of Frank's flashlight, the lads could see the imprint of a boot in a pitch of wet sand on the floor of the tunnel.

"Looks like a fresh track, too," said Joe.

"We're on the right trail. Let's keep moving."

With increasing excitement, the chums pressed forward and in a few moments Frank stepped out of the passage into another cave. This was the largest cave of all, an enormous underground vault, and even the flashlight beams failed to reveal the rocky walls and ceiling.

The floor was rough and broken fragments of rock were strewn about.

"Watch your step," warned Frank, as he made his way across the cave.

The others had flashlights and the floor was well illuminated as the boys slowly picked their way among the rocks. The far wall of the huge cavern was still invisible.

"This is a whopper!" said Joe, in an awed whisper.

Frank stopped, with a murmur of annoyance.

"What's the matter?" asked Chet.

"My flashlight. It's on the blink."

Vainly, Frank tried to coax a gleam from the

refractory instrument. It was no use. He put the light in his pocket.

"I'll have to fix it to-morrow," he said. "It won't work any more to-night by the looks of things."

"Here's mine," offered Biff.

But Frank declined.

"No thanks. One of you chaps take the lead for a while. I can follow easily enough."

Joe took the lead, as Frank suggested, and the little party moved on again.

It was rough going. The floor of the cave became piled high with rocks, evidently from cave-ins that had occurred in times past; in other parts it was pitted with little gullies and holes. In trying to avoid these, the chums gradually became separated.

Frank stumbled along behind. He felt the loss of his flashlight, but said nothing, relying on finding his way by the radiance provided by the lights carried by the others.

Soon, however, the three lights became scattered. Joe had gone to one side to avoid a huge boulder; Chet had gone to the other side and encountered a pit that prevented him from returning to Joe's trail; Biff had tried to follow Chet and had blundered into a labyrinth of rocks.

Frank stood uncertainly for a moment, then called out.

"We're getting separated. Wait for me."

The walls of the great cave flung back the echoes time and again.

He heard Joe shout:

"Where are you?"

Had it not been for the glow of Joe's light he would never have known where the voice came from because the echoes confused him, and the tones seemed to come from all parts of the cave.

Frank realized that his own shouts would cause the same confusion to the others.

"Don't move around!" he called. "I'll head toward one of the lights."

But evidently his order was misunderstood, for one of the lights began to move erratically through the darkness.

Frank went forward. He blundered against a rock and fell, bruising his knees. He got to his feet and went on, still in the direction of the nearest glow.

He was confused by the moving lights. Had his own flashlight not failed him this would not have happened.

Suddenly, he stumbled.

He lurched forward. His foot groped wildly for the firm rock, but there was nothing to stop his plunge. He had fallen into a pit.

Straight down through the blackness he hurtled, with a wild cry of terror.

The others heard that cry. They heard a far-off crash, and then the clatter of falling rock.

Joe was the first to shout.

"Frank!" he called.

There was no answer. The echoes rang back.

Although the other boys shouted time and again there was no answer from Frank Hardy. They searched frantically, casting the beams of their lights here and there, but they found no trace of him.

CHAPTER XIII

STOLEN SUPPLIES

THE other boys searched for nearly an hour, but Frank Hardy seemed to have disappeared literally into the bowels of the earth.

With only their flashlights to illuminate the huge cave, they found it difficult to conduct the search with any degree of satisfaction. They blundered here and there, not at all certain that they were anywhere near the place where their companion had disappeared.

They found several deep pits in the floor of the cave, natural crevices and holes in the rock, but although they shouted at the top of their lungs they heard no answering cry from below.

"He must have fallen down one of these holes, that's certain," Joe declared. "I'm sure we haven't missed any."

"Why doesn't he call back then?" said Biff.

In the glow of the flashlights the boys glanced at one another anxiously. Joe expressed the thought that the others were afraid to put into words.

"Perhaps he can't."

"Do you think he may be dead?" asked Chet quietly.

"We'll hope not," sighed Joe. "But when he doesn't answer, things don't look any too bright. Any of these crevices may be hundreds of feet deep, for all we know."

"It will be a terrible end to our trip if anything like that has happened."

"Not much use waiting for morning," declared Biff. "This cave is just as dark in the daytime as it is right now. I sure wish we had a few more flashlights."

"Or more powerful ones. We can't see very far down the crevices in the rocks, with these lights."

The boys talked in low tones. They were awed by the thought of what might have happened to Frank Hardy. In their ears still rang that last dreadful cry and they could still hear the crashing of rocks as their companion hurtled into the depths. Even now his mangled body might be lying in some subterranean pit from which it would be impossible to recover it. Joe shuddered.

They listened in vain for some faint cry. But there was nothing but the echoes of their own voices.

"We won't give up for a while yet," said Joe, with as much steadiness of voice as he could muster. "We'll search around every pit and hole we can find. I *can't* believe he was killed!"

Keeping close together, the lads slowly crossed the floor of the cave. When they reached an opening in the rocks they directed the beams of their three flashlights into the shadowy depths, thus gaining more radiance than had they been searching singly. Then they yelled and shouted.

There was no reply. The flashlights revealed only jagged walls of rock. There was no sign of Frank.

On to the next crevice. This, fortunately, was not deep, but although the lights revealed the bottom and although they played the triple beams along every inch of the floor of the subterranean ravine, there was no sight of a crumpled figure.

Patiently, they searched the cave, but at last they were forced to admit that they were at a standstill.

"Not much use going any farther just now," sighed Joe. "We need more light." He sat down moodily on a rock and buried his face in his hands.

"I wish we had never followed that fellow who was in the cave," said Chet. "Chances are, it has cost Frank his life."

"I'm not giving up hope yet," Joe declared. "There's a chance that he might have been knocked unconscious by his fall, and if we can only reach him in time we may be able to save him. But these flashlights aren't much help. We're just groping around in the dark."

"I have an idea," offered Biff.

"What is it?"

"Let's build a fire. It might light up the cave enough to show us what we are doing."

"How can we light a fire?" asked Chet. Then he looked up sharply. "You're right, Biff. I forgot that we have lots of wood in the outside cave."

"That's not a bad stunt!" declared Joe hopefully. "With a roaring bonfire in here we'll be able to light up the whole place and see what we're about."

"Let's get at it."

Biff's plan seemed valuable, but before leaving the cave in search of wood, the boys made a last attempt to locate their missing comrade, by shouting loudly. However, as before, there was not the faintest reply.

They made their way out into the next cave, and from there into the outer cavern where they had originally taken refuge from the storm. They were harassed by the thought that death might have overtaken their missing companion, and they said scarcely a word as they went about the business of gathering driftwood for the proposed bonfire.

Each of them took an armful of the wood and they were just about to return through the caves again when Joe noticed something that caused him to drop his wood on the floor with a clatter.

"What's wrong now?" asked Chet, in surprise.

"That's funny," Joe returned. "I was sure we left our supplies right near this woodpile."

"So we did," Biff assured him.

"They're not here now."

"They must be. I piled them there myself, all except a few that I put over by the other wall."

"Come and see for yourself."

Joe turned the beam of his flashlight on the place where Biff had stacked the greater part of their supplies. A loaf of bread and a tin of sardines lay on the rock, but that was all.

Biff's astonishment was so great that he could scarcely speak for a moment.

Then he gasped:

"They've been stolen!"

"All of 'em?" demanded Chet, in alarm. The loss of their provisions would be a serious matter to him.

"Where did you put the rest of the stuff, Biff?" asked Joe.

Biff turned his flashlight on the opposite wall. There the light revealed a few bundles and tins, the rest of the supplies.

"Well, they're safe, at any rate."

"But where are the others? They *can't* be stolen. They were here when we went to sleep."

"Must have been stolen while we were in the other caves," declared Chet.

"But who could have taken them?" exclaimed Joe.

"The chap who woke us up. I'll bet he didn't go into the other caves at all, or if he did he just hid himself until we passed. Then he came out and stole our food."

"Perhaps that's what he came for in the first place," suggested Biff.

Solemnly, the lads looked from the loaf of bread and the tin of sardines on the floor of the cave to the few things on the other side.

"He sure didn't leave much. This means we'll have to go back to the village," said Chet, a bit impatiently.

"We can't take time to worry about that now," Joe reminded him. "We have to keep up our search for Frank."

"That's right," agreed Biff. "It's tough to lose our food; but we have enough to last us another day, anyway, and it's more important to get Frank back than our supplies.''

''Of course it is,'' agreed Chet soberly.

The boys picked up their firewood again and, with Joe in the lead, went into the second cave, then on into the cavern where their chum had vanished. As they trudged on through the darkness, following the gleam of the flashlights, Chet and Biff wondered vainly about the thief who had disturbed them and robbed them. Joe's agonized thoughts circled about his vanished brother.

CHAPTER XIV

Captain Royal

When the three boys reached the cave where they had last seen Frank Hardy they piled the driftwood in a heap close by one of the pits in the floor.

They were surprised at the number of holes and crevices they had discovered.

"It's a wonder we weren't all killed," said Chet. "We were all prowling around this cave without any idea of the danger."

"It's a good place to stay out of," Joe remarked. "But first of all we'll try to get Frank out of it too."

He was trying to be hopeful, but it was difficult. The ominous silence since his brother's disappearance had been none too encouraging.

They lit the fire. In a short time, the flames flared high and a flickering radiance illuminated the cave, revealing the damp ceiling high above, the clammy walls in the distance, and the rough floor, seamed and pitted with cracks and holes in the rock.

Methodically, they resumed their search, investigating each of these gigantic crevices. But in spite of all their shouts, in spite of the fact that they were enabled to make a more thorough search now that the cave was not as dark as it had been, in spite of the fact that Joe even descended one of the shallower pits on the chance that Frank might be lying unconscious at the bottom, their search was in vain.

"I'm afraid it's no use," said Biff finally.

"I hate to give up!" declared Joe. "And yet—we've done all we can."

"Better have some sleep and try again tomorrow," Chet suggested. "Frank is either unconscious or—or dead. Some of these pits seem terribly deep."

Joe realized that the advice was reasonable. They were all very tired and in no condition to continue the search. As Chet said, if Frank were alive or conscious, he would have shouted to them.

"All right," agreed Joe. "We'll go back to the other cave. But I'm afraid I'll never be able to sleep."

"We'll have a rest, anyway. Then we'll come back. If we still can't find him we'll go back to the village and get some men to help us with ropes and big searchlights. We'll never go back to Bayport until we find out what has happened to him."

Disconsolately, the boys turned away.

They were almost at the entrance of the second cave when they heard a faint sound.

Joe wheeled about.

"What was that?"

They listened. The sound was repeated. It was like a distant cry.

"Somebody calling!" declared Biff excitedly.

"It must be Frank!"

The boys stood quite still and listened for a repetition of the call. It came again, muffled and far away, but unmistakably a human voice.

With one accord, they turned and ran back into the cave.

"It's Frank!"

They hurried across the treacherous floor in the direction of the sound. It was clearer now.

"Joe! Joe!"

They recognized Frank's voice.

The call came from a part of the cave that they had not searched carefully. Joe shouted back excitedly:

"We hear you, Frank! Call again, so we'll know where to find you!"

Again came the faint shout. It guided them toward a pit that was almost hidden from view by a huge boulder. It was one of the few pits that they had overlooked.

Evidently Frank had seen the reflection of their searchlights, for he shouted weakly:

"Right over here."

At the edge of the pit, they looked down.

There, just a blur in the gloom, they distinguished a figure. Frank was standing up, leaning against the side of the rocky shaft, just a few yards below.

Chet had brought with him a length of stout rope and he quickly flung one end of this down into the pit.

"We'll have you out of there in no time. Boy, but it's good to hear your voice again!" There was heartfelt relief in his tones.

Frank explained that the sides of the pit were too steep to enable him to make his way to the surface without assistance. However, with the aid of the rope, and with Joe and his chums pulling lustily, he was soon hauled to the top.

As he scrambled up out of the pit, the others noticed, in the glow of the fire, that he had a nasty gash across his temple.

"You're hurt!" said Joe, when the first exclamations of enthusiasm and delight had died down.

"I'm all right now," Frank assured them. "I'm a little dizzy yet, and weak, but it isn't serious."

"What happened?"

"I fell down the pit, and I struck my head against the rocks. It must have knocked me out for a few minutes but when I came to, I began to shout.''

"A few minutes!" exclaimed Chet. "We've been hunting for you over an hour."

Frank looked incredulous.

"An hour! Why, I thought I had been unconscious only a little while."

The others then told him of the search they had made and of their anxiety on his account. However, they were so relieved at seeing him safe and sound again that they soon forgot the serious side of the affair and Chet remarked that Frank had been lucky in having an hour's sleep while the rest had been shouting their lungs out. They trooped out of the cavern back toward their own cave, and Joe told his brother about the missing supplies.

"That's queer," said Frank. "Were they stolen while we were in the big cave?"

"It looks like that."

"But the man who woke us up went into the big cave ahead of us."

"He may have hidden and we might have passed him."

"That's possible. Perhaps it wasn't a man at all. The thief might have been an animal."

The others had not considered this explanation.

"No use crying over spilled milk now," declared Frank. "We'd just better go back to sleep and hunt for our supplies in the morning."

When morning came, a diligent search of the cave failed to reveal any clues that would help the boys trace the thief, whether man or animal.

"We're out of luck, that's all," concluded Frank finally. "Our friend must have fooled us nicely. Perhaps he came into the cave to steal supplies in the first place, then slipped past us in the darkness when we went to look for him."

"And helped himself," said Chet gloomily.

"He left something, at any rate. We won't starve to-day, and if our grub runs out we can go back to the village for more. We'll make the best of it. Let's start exploring the shoreline. That's what we came for."

The matter of the stolen supplies was thus dismissed, although Chet was very gloomy for some time as he thought of the food that had been taken, notably a tin of strawberry jam, of which he was inordinately fond.

The storm was over, and from the cave they could see the sun shining on the blue waters of the sea. They lost no time in eating breakfast and then hastening down to the beach. Although they were dubious as to the advisability of leaving their remaining supplies in the cave, they reasoned that as it was impossible to take the provisions everywhere with them, they would have to run the risk of further theft.

Out on the beach, beneath the lowering black cliffs, they forgot the unfortunate beginning of their quest in the delight of the keen, salty air and the cool breeze from the sea. The sandy shore wound about the face of a great bluff of black rock and when the lads had skirted this precipice they were confronted by a dark opening at the base of the cliff just a few yards away.

"Another cave!" exclaimed Frank.

Chet gave a cheer.

"Let's investigate."

They advanced on the cave, but when they were just in front of the entrance they halted with exclamations of surprise.

Tacked on a board stuck in the sand beside the cave mouth was a tattered fragment of paper. On it, in black letters scrawled with a heavy pencil, they read:

NO TRESPASSING.

The boys looked at this sign in astonishment.

"By order of the chief of police," murmured Chet, with a grin.

"Looks as if somebody has been here before," Biff observed.

"Perhaps somebody just put up the sign for a joke. Let's take a peep inside."

Frank advanced toward the cave.

But at the entrance he paused. He peered into the gloomy beyond and then turned back to his companions.

"The sign isn't a joke," he said quietly. "Somebody lives here!"

"*Lives* there!" ejaculated Chet incredulously.

"Come and see for yourself."

Curiously, the lads crowded into the entrance of the cave. They saw at a glance that Frank was right. In the gloomy interior of the cave they could see a crude table, a mattress with blankets, and on a ledge of rock was an improvised cupboard consisting of an old soap box. That the cave had only been recently tenanted they saw by the fact that the box held some canned goods and some other provisions that had certainly not been there long.

"Well, I'll be switched!" declared Joe. "We have a neighbor."

"We certainly have. And if I'm not mistaken, here he comes now."

Frank was looking down the beach. The others turned.

"What a queer duck he is!" exclaimed Biff.

"I'll say he is!" ejaculated Chet Morton. "Where do they get 'em like that?"

Coming around a jutting promontory of rock was a queer old man, clad in fisherman's garb, with a huge straw hat on his head. He had not seen them as yet. He was singing, in a high-pitched voice, and even at that distance they could make out the words:

"I'm Captain Royal, of the King's Navee,
And I want two lumps of sugar in my tea."

CHAPTER XV

THE OLD SAILOR

HAVING concluded this verse, the strange old man elevated one arm above his head and danced a couple of steps of a sailor's hornpipe. In the middle of this he caught sight of the boys, and came to an abrupt stop.

"Ahoy!" he shouted.

"Ahoy!" cried Chet promptly.

The man in the straw hat advanced.

"When did you come ashore?"

"Just this morning."

The old man drew closer. He was an odd figure, in the flopping straw hat, with oilskins much too big for him, and as he came up to the mouth of the cave he looked closely at the lads, then smiled and extended his hand.

"I'm Captain Royal," he announced. "You should have saluted, but I guess you didn't know."

To make up for this breach of etiquette, the boys saluted, and this appeared to gratify the old gentleman immensely.

116

"You're landlubbers, eh?"

"I suppose so," admitted Frank, with a smile.

"Well, we can't all be sailors. It isn't often people come to see me."

"Do you live here?" asked Joe, indicating the cave.

"This is where I live when I'm ashore. I'm resting up between cruises just now."

The old man sat down on the sand and fanned himself with the straw hat, for it was a warm morning and the sun was strong. The boys looked at him curiously. In spite of his garb, he did not look like a sea-faring man; his skin was tanned, it is true, but it was not the deep, mahogany tan of one who has lived for years in many climes. His voice was high-pitched and his expression was mild. But the boys were old enough to know that one cannot always judge by appearances.

"What are your names?" asked the old man.

The lads introduced themselves.

"Glad to meet you," returned Captain Royal. "It ain't often I have visitors. I get used to being alone."

"It's lonely enough here," agreed Frank.

"It isn't bad. Not half as lonely as the time I got marooned in the South Seas."

The boys looked at him with new interest.

"You were marooned?"

"Aye. It was when I was in charge of a destroyer cruising the South Seas a good many years ago. We landed for water on a little island that you won't find on any of the maps. It was a hot day—very hot. Must have been over a hundred degrees in the shade. So while my men were loading the water on my boat I sat down in the shade of a cactus tree. Before I knew it, I was asleep."

"And they went away and left you?"

"They did."

"But you were the captain!"

"I guess they thought I was in my cabin, and of course none of 'em dared disturb me. When I woke up, the ship was gone."

"Gosh!" exclaimed Biff.

"Well, sir, I didn't know what to do. I was like this here fellow Robinson Crusoe, that you read about. But I had to make the best of it, so I fixed myself up a little house and I lived there for nearly six months, all by myself."

"Didn't the boat come back for you?"

"They couldn't find the island again. It wasn't marked on the maps. The engineer couldn't set a course back to the island. Anyway, the quartermaster who took charge of the schooner after they found I was gone, didn't want to find me, I guess. He wanted my job."

"How did you find anything to eat when you were on the island?"

"Oh, there was lots to eat. Cocoanuts and prunes and bananas and grapefruit and figs and all sorts of fruit. There was plenty of mud-turtles on the island, so I had mock turtle soup whenever I wanted it. I tell you, I lived high. Once in a while I had my little troubles, of course, and two or three times I had some mighty narrow escapes. There was a rhinoceros came after me once."

"A rhinoceros!"

"Aye! He swam up to the island one day. I was just in for my morning swim when I saw his big ears flapping and heard him give a roar. I tell you, I was scared. He came surging through the waves and up on the beach and he chased me clean up a pineapple tree. I had to stay there for three days until he went away, and I had nothing but pineapples to eat. I was never so sick of pineapples in my life. I've never been able to eat one since."

Frank glanced at his brother. He was beginning to suspect that Captain Royal was having some fun at their expense. The old man rattled on.

"The rhinoceros finally swam out to sea again and I was able to come down. I lived on that island for half a year, hoping that my warship would come back, but it never did. So I made myself a raft and loaded it up with water and fruit and finally sailed away. It took me more than a month of steady sailing before I finally reached land off the coast of South America. By jing, I was glad when I saw the Andes Mountains again. I landed at a port where there was a ship, and I'm swizzled if it wasn't my own boat.''

"Your own boat!"

"Yes sir. I could hardly believe my eyes. So I come on board, and they were going to throw me off.''

"Why?" asked Chet, in surprise.

"They didn't know me. You see, I hadn't been able to shave when I was on the island, and I'd grown a beard. So nobody knew me and they wouldn't believe me when I said I was their captain. But I told them to lend me a pair of scissors and a razor and I took off that beard and stepped out on deck, and by jing they all saluted me then, I can tell you. I made the quartermaster walk the plank and we all sailed back to San Francisco.''

"That was quite an adventure," said Frank politely.

"Oh, I've had many things happen to me. I've been in a lot of battles, too. Of course, I've retired from the navy now, for there isn't the excitement nowadays.''

"Were you in the Spanish-American war?" asked Chet.

"I was all through it from start to finish. I

had a narrow escape during that war. I took my ship out one night off the Philippines to see if I could catch a Spanish warship that I'd heard was in the neighborhood, and we sighted her just about midnight, not half a mile away. So we pumped a couple of shots over her keel and she turned and went steaming away to the north. Well, I gave chase, but the Spaniard was fast and it was three hours before we came alongside. We were just going to board the ship when the steward came up to me and said some other boats were coming up. There was. Five of 'em. All Spanish."

"What did you do?"

"What could I do? I couldn't run away. I told my men to get on board the Spaniard and I took all the sailors from that boat and made 'em surrender and put 'em on my ship. So the other boats didn't dare fire at my ship for fear of killing their own men and they didn't dare fire at the boat I was on for fear of sinking their own ship. So we opened fire on them and they didn't dare fire a shot back."

"That was mighty clever."

"Wasn't it? I sunk two of the Spaniards and the others surrendered and I brought 'em back to Manila Bay. I was given a medal for that."

Captain Royal looked very pleased with himself, and he dug into a capacious pocket and produced a plug of tobacco, taking a huge bite.

"Oh, I've had experiences," he said, wagging his head. "Are you going to be around here long?"

"Just a few days."

"I'd invite you to come and live in my cave, only there ain't much room."

"We have a cave of our own, farther down the shore."

"That's fine. I'll call and see you some time."

"We'll be glad to have you do that," said Joe cordially.

The old man got up and walked toward the entrance of his own cave.

"Come on inside," he urged. "You'd better stay and have some dinner with me. I was out fishing this morning and I caught quite a few fish. As soon as they're ready, we'll sit down and eat."

The boys accepted the invitation eagerly, and trooped into the cave of Captain Royal. Chet looked around hungrily for the fish, but there was none in sight. The old man invited them to sit down, and they squatted in the sand, there being no chairs or boxes.

"Are you the only person living around here, Captain Royal?" asked Frank.

"The only one. I thought I was the only person who knew about these caves until I saw you lads here.''

''There was some one visited us last night—'' began Frank. Then he hesitated in surprise, for Captain Royal leaped to his feet, a look of fear on his face.

''What's that?'' he exclaimed. ''Some one visited you! Don't tell me there's some one else around here!''

CHAPTER XVI

"Go Away!"

"Some one came into our cave last night and stole most of our supplies," said Frank.

"A man?"

"We didn't see him, but it could scarcely have been an animal of any kind, for he carried off a whole box of food."

"You don't say!" exclaimed Captain Royal.

"And we found a footprint too," added Joe.

Captain Royal shook his head in amazement.

"This is very strange. I had no idea there was any one else around this part of the coast. You can see for yourself that it is hard to get here, and if there were any one else around I would be sure to see him."

"And you've seen no one?"

"Not a living soul, besides yourselves. And he stole your supplies?"

"Nearly all of them. He left us some canned beans, a loaf of bread, some butter and some coffee; but that's about all."

"Canned beans! It's a long time since I've

had any canned beans. Perhaps we could trade."

"That's not a bad idea," said Chet. "There are other things we need."

"I have some dried fish here," said the captain. "I have fish and a case of eggs and some other things. Go get those beans and we'll trade."

Chet hastened back to the other cave and returned in due time with the cans of beans, which the captain accepted with considerable delight. In exchange, the boys received some fish and two dozen eggs.

"I got the eggs off a boat yesterday," explained Captain Royal, "and I've been thinking ever since that it was foolish of me to buy a whole case, because they mightn't keep. I'd rather have canned beans any day."

When the exchange was effected, their host suddenly became silent and sat for a long time looking gloomily at the sand. The boys were wondering when the promised fish dinner was to put in its appearance. Apparently, Captain Royal had forgotten all about his invitation. Suddenly he looked up.

"Well," he demanded curtly, "what are you hanging around for, boys?"

They gazed at the man in surprise.

"Why—you asked us to stay," stammered Frank.

"Yes," returned the old man tartly, "but I didn't ask you to stay all day."

The boys were so astonished at this sudden change of front that for a moment they thought the captain was joking. But they soon learned that he was in earnest, for he got to his feet with a mutter.

"Must I order you out?"

"Why, what's the matter?" inquired Joe. "Have we offended you in any way?"

"Be off with you! Go away! Get out of here."

The boys got to their feet, vastly surprised.

"Go away!" repeated Captain Royal, advancing on them with a threatening gesture. "Clear out. I prefer to be alone."

"Why, certainly," said Frank. "We had no idea we were disturbing you, Captain."

"Don't argue. Get out. By jing, I've had enough people bothering me lately and I'm not going to stand for it any longer. I thought when I found this cave that people would leave me alone, and now I am annoyed by a pack of meddlesome boys. Go away!"

Without further ado, the lads retreated from the cave. Captain Royal stood in the entrance, shaking his fist at them angrily.

"Clear out of here!" he stormed. "Don't let me catch you around this cave again or it will be the worse for you."

Then he wheeled about abruptly and disappeared into the darkness of the cave.

The boys looked at one another in amazement.

"Can you beat that!" exclaimed Chet.

"What's wrong with the old coot, anyway?" demanded Biff. "Has he gone crazy?"

"I can't understand it," said Frank. "One minute he invites us to stay for dinner, and in the next breath he orders us away."

Joe tapped his head significantly.

"I think he's a little bit off his head."

"Perhaps it's the heat," volunteered Chet.

"He is certainly a queer old codger," Biff declared. "I don't know what to make of him."

The boys went back down the beach toward their own cave. Fortunately, before he started, Chet had had enough presence of mind to pick up the provisions they had obtained from the old man, so the boys were so much to the good, at any rate.

"He's crazy," insisted Joe. "Those stories he told us were the wildest yarns I ever heard in my life. I wonder if he thought we were simple enough to believe them."

"As if anybody didn't know that a rhinoceros couldn't swim the ocean!" scoffed Chet.

"And pineapples that grow on a tree!"

"I don't think he's ever been a sailor at all,"

Frank declared. "His naval terms were certainly mixed. He called his ship a destroyer and a warship and a schooner and didn't seem to notice the difference. And he said the quartermaster was in charge after he left the ship."

"And everybody knows they don't make people walk the plank nowadays."

"His stories were as full of holes as a sieve. But I don't know whether he told them just for the fun of stuffing us or just because he is clean crazy and doesn't know any better."

The boys discussed Captain Royal and his eccentric behavior all the way back to their cave, and agreed that if the old gentleman was not a lunatic he was at least slightly unbalanced.

"The very fact that he lives away off here all by himself proves it," insisted Joe. "No man in his right mind would live in a cave down in this lonely spot. I wonder if he was the man who came and stole our supplies last night."

Frank shook his head.

"I thought of that and I took a look around his cave, but there was no sign of any of our stuff. Besides, he seemed much surprised when we told him there was some one else hanging around."

"He might have been smart enough to act

as though he were surprised. Perhaps he had
our provisions hidden away."

"But why would he want to trade with us?"

"Because he's crazy."

The lads went back to their own cave and
then went for a swim in the surf, forgetting
Captain Royal in their enjoyment of the stimu-
lating salt water. In spite of the generally
rocky nature of the coast the beach in front
of their cave was sandy and sloped gently into
the water, providing an ideal bathing place.

When the swim was over they prepared lunch
from what limited food they had on hand, and
in the afternoon they went back down the shore
again to resume their tour of exploration.

They did not see the captain again, although
they passed his cave, keeping at a respectful
distance so as not to incur his wrath. Farther
down the shore they found a series of large
caves, and some of these they explored. However, they found nothing of interest, although
they spent the entire afternoon prowling
about the caverns. At sundown they returned,
footsore and weary, to their own headquarters.

After supper they sat about their campfire
chatting, but Chet and Biff were so tired that
their heads soon began to nod and they decided
to retire for the night. Joe would have done
likewise, but Frank asked him to sit up a while
longer.

Biff and Chet were soon snoring, and not until then did Frank broach the subject on his mind.

"Did you notice an expression Captain Royal used several times when he was talking to us?" he asked his brother.

Joe reflected.

"I can't say that I noticed anything in particular," he confessed.

"Don't you remember that he said 'by jing' now and then?"

Joe looked up, startled.

"Now I remember! Yes, he did say that. And 'by jing' is the very expression—"

"The very expression Evangeline Todd said her missing brother used so often!"

"That's a fact!" exclaimed Joe. "And now that I come to think of it, I remember his shoe-laces."

"They were untied."

"And Todham Todd had a habit of going about with his shoelaces untied too!"

CHAPTER XVII

The Man on the Shore

The Hardy boys looked at one another solemnly in the glow of the campfire.

"Do you think Captain Royal and Todham Todd are one and the same man?" asked Joe.

"What do you think of it yourself?"

"It certainly looks strange. But how *could* this queer old chap be Todham Todd? How would the college professor get away down among these caves, and what would be his idea in passing himself off as a sea captain?"

Frank was thoughtful.

"Stranger things have happened. You remember that Evangeline Todd suggested that her brother might have lost his memory. He was always more or less eccentric, no doubt, and if he was suffering from amnesia there is no telling where he might go or what he might do."

"It's mighty strange if we have run across him in this place. Perhaps it's just a coincidence that Captain Royal says 'by jing' once

in a while. As for having his shoelaces untied, he seems pretty sloppy anyway, and that
would be only natural.''

''Oh, yes, there's every chance in the world
that Captain Royal is simply an eccentric old
tar. I agree with you there. Just the same,
we can't afford to overlook the chance that
he *might* be Todham Todd.''

''How are we going to find out?''

''If we asked him, he would deny it, certainly.
But perhaps if we could talk to him and ask
a few questions he might give himself away.''

''If he has lost his memory he would not remember anything to give away.''

''I hadn't thought of that,'' admitted Frank.
''Still, my plan is worth trying, don't you
think?''

''It certainly is. But do you think he'll talk
to us at all, after what happened to-day?''

''Perhaps he's forgotten all about it by now.
He might be as nice as pie if we went back.''

''Yes, he seems a rather changeable old boy,''
laughed Joe. ''And perhaps if he isn't around
we might find some clue in that cave of his.''

''Good idea. We'll make a try at it to-
morrow.''

''Do you think we should tell Chet and
Biff?'' asked Joe.

''I don't think so. Not just yet. After all,
they don't know about the Todd affair, and if

we find out that our suspicions are all wrong there'll be no harm done and they'll be none the wiser."

"But how can we question him if they're with us?"

"We'll make some excuse to get away by ourselves. Of course, we may be disappointed. The more I think of it the more impossible it seems that Todham Todd should actually be living here. But it is strange that he hasn't been found before this if he is living in any town or city where people would meet him and talk about him.

"Dad said he was traced as far as Claymore and there the trail vanished. Claymore isn't very far from this coast."

"That's right. He may have wandered down to these caves."

"How about the shooting and the mysterious lights we were warned about?"

Frank laughed.

"Oh, as to that," he said, "I think Captain Royal has just been having a little fun at the expense of the people around here. Perhaps he is trying to keep people from finding out too much about him."

"Well, we'll find out all we can, anyway. He can't scare us."

Having decided to investigate the eccentric old gentleman further, the Hardy boys rolled themselves up in their blankets and went to sleep. Frank hardly dared hope that his surmise was correct and that in Captain Royal they had discovered the missing college professor, but he was convinced that the old man was not a sailor, in spite of his claims, and the circumstances of the exclamation "by jing" and the untied shoelaces, slender as the clues were, led him to believe that they were at least on a trail worth following.

When the boys awakened next morning they found the sea hidden by a dense fog. It was damp and cold and the weather put all idea of further exploration of the coast out of their heads.

"I'm not going to wander among the rocks in this fog," declared Chet emphatically. "If it got worse we'd have a fine time finding our way back here."

"Looks to me like a good morning for fishing," said Biff.

Chet greeted this suggestion with enthusiasm.

"That's the brightest idea you've had in years. We brought lots of tackle with us, thank goodness, and there's a high rock over there that hangs over deep water. Perhaps we could catch a whale or so for lunch."

Frank and Joe saw their opportunity. They encouraged their two chums to go fishing. As for themselves, they said they would go down to Captain Royal's cave and see if the old gentleman was in a better humor than he had been the previous day.

"You're welcome," said Chet. "I've had enough of that old lad's society to last me the rest of my life. He'll probably set his dog on you, if he has one."

"I didn't see any dog there yesterday," grinned Joe.

"Well, he'll likely have a dogfish then. You want to be careful. Better come fishing with us."

But the Hardy boys persisted in their determination to beard the lion in his den again, as Frank put it, so Biff and Chet unpacked the fishing tackle and made their plans for a morning's sport.

After breakfast they set out for the high rock, Chet ironically asking the Hardy boys to give his love to Captain Royal, and Frank and Joe started off down the beach, delighted that they had escaped so easily.

They proceeded along the beach. The fog hung low over the sea and it was so dense that they could scarcely distinguish the outline of the dark cliffs above.

"Not much chance of catching Captain Royal away from home to-day, I'm thinking," said Frank.

"No, he's likely sitting in his cosy little cave beside a good fire. Well, he may feel more like talking."

There was no breeze blowing, and the sea lay calm and slatey beneath the fog. It was a damp, clammy morning and the chill penetrated to the bone. The boys felt rather guilty at having left Chet and Biff, to set out on this expedition of their own, but as Frank had pointed out it was, after all, private business. They well knew that if their suspicions were incorrect, Chet would joke about the affair unmercifully. It was better to keep it to themselves until they were certain of their ground.

They were just approaching the cliff that hid Captain Royal's cave from view when Frank halted and peered through the fog at the base of the rocks some distance ahead.

"Do you see somebody lying there, Joe?"

Joe looked in the direction he indicated.

"Looks like an old log—no, it moved!"

"Seems like a man sprawled on the sand."

"Perhaps it's Captain Royal. Maybe he fell and hurt himself."

The boys hastened across the rocks in the direction of the figure on the shore.

As they drew nearer they saw that it was indeed a man who lay sprawled at the base of the rocks, apparently asleep. However, they soon saw that it was not Captain Royal.

"Perhaps somebody fell off the cliffs from above," ventured Joe, as they hastened up to the recumbent figure.

Frank looked up. The cliff loomed high above.

"If he did, we can't help him now. He would be dead."

They came up to the man sprawled on the sand. He was not dead. An empty bottle lying by his side told the reason for his slumber.

"He's drunk!"

The man's face was turned away from them and the boys could not distinguish his features. He was roughly dressed and his clothes were wet with fog.

Just then the fellow stirred restlessly in his drunken sleep. He slowly turned his head.

When the boys saw his face they gasped with surprise.

"It's Carl Schaum!" exclaimed Frank.

It was indeed the escaped automobile thief, the man who had stolen Frank's motorcycle the day the boys left Bayport.

CHAPTER XVIII

The Prisoner

Carl Schaum did not awaken. His slumber was too deep. He was quite senseless from the effects of the liquor he had drunk.

"This is luck!" exclaimed Frank. "I wonder how he got here!"

"I suppose he's hiding down in these caves away from the police."

Something beside the bottle near the slumbering man caught Frank's eye. He bent forward and examined it.

It was a small package containing several tins of meat, of the same variety the Hardy boys and their chums had brought with them on their expedition to the caves.

"There's our thief!" Frank declared, with conviction. "It was Carl Schaum who stole the provisions from our cave."

There seemed little doubt that this was the case. The evidence of the package of food was conclusive.

"What shall we do with him?" asked Joe.

Frank groped in his pocket and produced a length of stout cord.

"We'll tie him up first. He's an escaped criminal and it's our duty to turn him over to the police."

"What if he puts up a fight?"

"He's too drunk. Anyway, we should be more than a match for him."

They looked at the man sprawled on the ground. He was snoring loudly, quite oblivious of his danger. Quietly, the Hardy boys took up their positions, one on each side of the fellow, and then with a quick movement they turned him over on his back and pinned his arms behind him.

To their surprise, Carl Schaum did not struggle. He merely groaned in his sleep.

"He's dead drunk," said Frank. "We won't have any trouble with him."

Quickly he flipped the cord about Carl Schaum's wrists, and they bound the unconscious man. Still he did not awaken. When the boys were satisfied that their captive was firmly trussed up they stood back to await further developments.

Carl Schaum snored on.

"I guess we'd better wake him up," said Frank, with a mischievous grin.

"It would take a cannon to waken him, by the looks of things."

"Good cold water should do the trick."

Frank went down to the shore, took off his hat and dipped it in the sea. He hastened back, the hat half full of water, and dashed it in Carl Schaum's face.

There was a splutter. Then Joe, anxious to be in on the fun, filled his hat and flung a copious supply of cold water at their captive.

Carl Schaum blinked, groaned, spluttered again, and tried to sit up.

"This will make us even for stealing my motorcycle," said Frank, as he dashed more water into the fellow's face.

"And this," said Joe, hastening up with another hatful.

Carl Schaum was literally drenched. He opened his eyes, then gave vent to a strangled yell. Frank managed to fling another hatful of water into his face before the boys decided that their captive was sufficiently awake.

"Hey! What's this?" roared Schaum indignantly. He had just discovered that his wrists were bound.

"Just a little joke," said Frank.

Water was streaming down the man's face. He was thoroughly aroused by now.

He was still too dazed to recognize the Hardy boys. As he sat on the beach, with his wet hair down over his eyes, his clothes completely soaked, he was a ridiculous object, and his expression of mingled wrath and surprise made it difficult for the lads to restrain their laughter.

"Lemme go!" demanded Schaum, struggling to release his wrists, without success.

Frank shook his head.

"Nothing doing. You're wanted back in Bayport, Schaum, and that is where you're going."

Schaum gasped.

"Bayport!" he said, after a moment. "Where's that? I never heard of the place."

"Oh, yes you have. You escaped from the Bayport jail, Schaum, and they'll be glad to see you back again."

"You're crazy!" the rascal stormed. "I was never in any jail!"

"How about the stolen automobiles on the Shore Road?"

"And Gus Montrose and the others in the gang?"

Carl Schaum saw that his bluff had failed. Then he looked more closely at the brothers. He turned pale.

"The Hardy boys!" he exclaimed.

"At your service," returned Joe, with a bow.

"You see, we know what we're talking about Get up, Schaum."

"What are you going to do with me?"

"Get up!" repeated Frank. "We're going

to take you out to the road and see that you're
turned over to the authorities.''

"Don't do that," whined Schaum. "Honest,
I never had anything to do with stealing them
cars. Let me go.''

"You were in the gang, and if they've been
punished, it isn't fair that you should get off,''
insisted Frank. "You escaped from the jail
and if you are innocent you had nothing to
fear. You'd better get up and come with us.''

He prodded the prisoner firmly with the toe
of his heavy tramping shoe, and Schaum
struggled to his feet. He made many whining
pleas for mercy, but the Hardy boys were determined that he should be sent back to Bayport to answer for his participation in the
Shore Road automobile thefts.

"I've reformed," sniveled Schaum. "I've
gone straight ever since I got out of jail.''

"Yes, you have!" laughed Frank. "How
about stealing my motorcycle while we were
in swimming?''

Schaum looked confused.

"I didn't know it was your motorcycle.''

"It doesn't matter whose motorcycle it was.
You meant to steal it. That doesn't look as if
you've reformed very much. No, you must
come along with us.''

Unwillingly, Carl Schaum stumbled along
the beach with his two captors.

Frank and Joe did not have a very clear idea of what they were to do with Schaum, now that they had captured him. At first they thought of keeping him in the cave, but Joe pointed out that he might get away again and that it would mean too much trouble keeping guard over him.

"And he'd eat too much," added Frank. "That's another little score we have to settle with you, Schaum. You were in the cave the other night and stole most of our provisions."

"I was hungry," whined the prisoner. "I only meant to borrow a little bit of food."

"Borrowers don't come sneaking around when every one is asleep. Where are our provisions now?"

"They're in my own cave," said Schaum sullenly.

"Where is that?"

"Try to find it."

"All right," returned Frank. "When you go back to Bayport you will find yourself facing an extra charge of robbery. We'll lay a complaint against you for stealing our provisions. You've already admitted that you took them, so it will go hard with you."

Schaum wilted at this threat.

"Aw, don't tell on me," he begged. "Your grub is all right. It's in the cave that you'll find not ten feet from where I was lying on the beach. I got to drinking last night and I wandered out of the cave and fell down.''

''I'm glad you've decided to be sensible,'' observed Frank. ''We'll go to the cave and get our food when we come back. We didn't know you had a cave.''

''I came here just a little while before you boys came.''

''Did you bring your trunk?'' asked Frank, with a grin. ''Anything in your cave you'd like to take back to jail with you?''

Schaum shook his head.

''No,'' he answered shortly. ''Just a pair of blankets. You can have 'em.''

''They'll give you blankets in jail.''

The boys soon reached their own cave. There was no sign of Chet and Biff, and they realized that the fishers might be far off down the shore by now, so they decided to take Carl Schaum out to the road themselves.

They clambered up the trail through the ravine until they reached the top of the cliff, and then they made their way over the rocks and down the hillside back to the fisherman's cottage. The fisherman was at home, and when he saw the little procession coming down the path he rushed out, anxious to learn what had happened. He was greatly excited when he saw that the villainous-looking Carl Schaum was bound.

"Have you cotched the man who was firin'
off all the guns?" he asked.

Frank shook his head.

"I don't think this is he," he said, remembering that Schaum had reached the caves only
a short time in advance of their own arrival.
"But he's almost as bad."

"What's he been doin'?"

The Hardy boys explained why they had
captured Carl Schaum, and when the fisherman
learned that they were going to take their
captive out to the main road he promptly volunteered the use of his car, an ancient and
decrepit flivver. The boys had been wondering
how they would get Schaum out to the road
by motorcycle, and the fisherman's offer solved
this difficulty.

Accordingly, they all wedged themselves into
the ramshackle car and set out for the main
road, which they reached in due time. Frank
and Joe did not want to waste too much time
with Schaum, and they decided to wait in hope
that some passing motorist would take the fellow in to the nearest police station.

In a short time a car came into sight and when
it came near, Frank stepped out into the road
and signaled the driver to stop. The automobile slowed down.

The man at the wheel looked at them curiously.

Then Frank gave an exclamation of delight.
"Why, he's from Bayport!" he shouted to
Joe. "It's Mr. Simms."

At the same moment, the driver recognized
Frank.

"Hello there, Hardy!" he exclaimed. "What
are you doing so far away from home?"

Frank and Joe knew Mr. Simms, having met
him at the time of the solving of the Shore
Road mystery, because he was one of the automobile owners who had suffered at the hands
of the car thieves. The very car Mr. Simms
was driving just then had been recovered by
the Hardy boys when they had found the automobiles stolen by Gus Montrose, Carl Schaum
and the other members of the gang.

"This is luck!" exclaimed Frank. "How
would you like to take a passenger back to Bayport with you?"

"Do you want a ride?" asked Mr. Simms.
"Hop in."

"I'm not asking for myself. But our friend
here is wanted back in Bayport. Perhaps you
could take him in."

Mr. Simms looked doubtfully at Carl Schaum.

"Well," he said slowly, "if he's a friend
of yours, I suppose it's all right—"

He had noticed that Schaum's wrists were
tied.

Frank laughed.

"I was just joking. This is one of the fellows who stole your car last month. Carl Schaum—"

"Oh! The thief that escaped, eh?"

"Yes. We ran across him down along the shore, and we were anxious to turn him over to the police again."

"Put him in the car," said Simms grimly. "I'll put the rascal where he belongs."

Rejoiced at having the prisoner taken off their hands so readily, the Hardy boys bundled Schaum into the rear seat of the automobile. They apologized to Mr. Simms for troubling him, but the man assured them that it was no trouble at all.

"It's a pleasure," he said. "I'll see that he doesn't get away." He glared at Carl Schaum. "So you're one of the scoundrels who stole my car, are you? And you thought you were going to escape a term in jail! You'll have to be mighty smart to do it then, for I'm going to break a few speed records getting you back to Bayport. I'm going to enjoy this trip."

He waved good-bye to the Hardy boys.

"I don't know how you caught him," he said; "but I'll tell the Bayport police to give you the credit. I'm certainly glad I came along in time to drive this guy back to jail, where he belongs."

With that he drove off and in a few minutes

he was carrying out his promise to break speed records on the way back to Bayport, while the helpless prisoner in the back seat was jounced and bounced until his teeth rattled.

Frank and Joe grinned.

"I guess Carl Schaum won't forget that ride for a while."

"Serves the rogue right!" declared the fisherman.

"Well, let's be getting back," said Frank. "The morning is almost gone and we haven't called on Captain Royal yet."

CHAPTER XIX

Clippings

THEIR friend, the fisherman, was greatly interested in the Hardy boys' adventure with Carl Schaum and wanted to know all the details of the affair. Frank and Joe told him why they had captured Schaum, and also told him of the Shore Road automobile thefts, although they modestly omitted any mention of their own part in bringing the car thieves to justice.

When they arrived back at the cottage the fisherman was anxious that they go in and continue the chat, but the Hardy boys wanted to return to the caves.

"Some other time," they promised.

"Well," said the fisherman reluctantly, "if you won't come in, I suppose you won't; but you must come back and see me before you leave these parts. You're smart lads, cotchin' that jailbird, and I'm sure he's the fellow that's been performin' all the monkeyshines down around Honeycomb Caves."

Frank and Joe said nothing. It occurred to them that possibly the fisher folk did not know of Captain Royal's presence in the vicinity and they preferred to keep the secret to themselves.

"Yes," said the man, wagging his head, "I guess he was the chap, all right, even if you don't seem to think so."

"He was a thief, at any rate," said Joe.

"He stole your grub, you was sayin'. If you need more, you're welcome to anything I've got here. It ain't much, but your more'n welcome," said their hospitable friend.

The boys thanked him, but assured him that Carl Schaum had been forced to divulge the hiding place of the provisions. With great glee they told how they had frightened him into telling.

"We're all set for a few days' stay now," said Frank. "I guess we won't be bothered any more."

The boys parted from the fisherman and ascended the path up the hillside again. Up over the rocks, along the cliff edge until they came to the ravine, down the steep slope, and after an arduous hour they were again at their cave.

Chet and Biff were nowhere to be seen, so the Hardy boys assumed that they were still fishing.

"When we tell them all the adventures we've had, they'll be as mad as hops," laughed Frank.

"We've sure covered a lot of territory since they last saw us."

"And the day isn't over yet. We still have Captain Royal to attend to."

It was still damp and foggy as they went on down the beach, and although it was midday the mist hung so heavily over the sea that they could see only a short distance ahead. It was almost as dark as at dusk.

"I believe the fog is growing worse," remarked Frank.

"It certainly seems worse since we've got down on the shore again."

"I hope Chet and Biff don't get lost."

"Not much danger of getting lost around here. It's pretty hard to get far from the ocean, and once you're on the beach you just have to keep walking until you find the caves."

The boys came to the place where they had spied Carl Schaum in his drunken slumber.

"Let's see if he was telling us the truth about that cave of his," Joe suggested. "We might as well make sure that our provisions are safe."

"There's a cave here, all right. Look, I can see it over by those big boulders."

"So there is. Queer that we didn't notice it before. The rocks hide it from view unless you stand right in front of it."

"Trust Carl to pick a good hiding place. If he hadn't made the mistake of getting drunk and wandering beyond his own front door, he might be a free man yet.''

''It isn't the first time that liquor has landed a man in jail.''

The boys approached the entrance of the cave. It was, as Joe had pointed out, almost invisible from the beach, unless one happened to look up when standing directly in front of the opening, because a number of huge boulders obscured it.

Inside, they found unmistakable evidences of human habitation.

''There are our provisions!'' exclaimed Frank.

He pointed to a box that stood beside a few blankets in a corner of the little cave. It was filled with the food that Schaum had stolen from them. Very little of it had been touched; the robber had been given no time to dispose of his loot.

''Well, I never expected to see *that* again,'' said Joe.

''I guess it's safe enough where it is. We can pick it up on our way back from Captain Royal's.''

''How about these blankets? Schaum said we could have them.''

Frank picked up one of the blankets. It was heavy and of excellent quality.

''I'll say he was mighty generous, letting us

have good blankets like these," he declared.
"They seem brand new, too."

"If they are, there must be a catch in it
somewhere."

"There is. Look!"

Frank held out the blanket. Stamped into
the fabric was the name, "Hotel Bayport."
The reason for Schaum's sudden burst of gen-
erosity was now clear.

"No wonder he didn't want to take them
with him. He knew that if the police laid eyes
on those blankets he'd have another charge
laid against him. He must have stolen them
from the hotel after he escaped from jail."

"I think he would take anything that wasn't
nailed down," said Joe. "Well, we can take
the blankets back with us and return them to
the hotel, at any rate."

"Sure. We'll leave 'em here with the grub
until we're ready to go back to our own cave."

The boys found nothing else worthy of attention in Carl Schaum's crude abode except
a revolver hidden beneath a rock near the blankets. They appropriated this, to turn over to
the police when they should return to Bayport.

They departed, well satisfied with their visit.

"Chet will give three cheers when he sees the
grub again. I don't think he was very cheerful about the thought of going on short ra-
tions until we got new supplies," said Frank.

"I wasn't very cheerful about it myself," Joe admitted. "It makes me sore when I think of Schaum stealing all that stuff. Why, one man couldn't eat it all in a month."

"Perhaps he intended to stay a month, or even longer, if he could get away with it."

"Well, he might have left us more than he did. I'm glad I was able to douse some water in his face."

The Hardy boys were soon in sight of Captain Royal's cave. The gloomy opening was barely visible through the lowering mist.

"I wonder if the old gentleman could be at home, Joe."

"No sign of life around, anyway."

"Perhaps he's asleep."

They made their way to the cave-mouth, cautiously. Still there was no sign of the captain.

"Better call him," suggested Frank.

They halted.

"Captain Royal!" shouted Joe.

There was no answer.

"I guess he's not at home."

They called out Captain Royal's name again, but still there was no reply, so they ventured close to the cave-mouth and peeped inside. The place was deserted.

"Shall we go in?" said Joe.

"Sure. We'll take a look around."

They stepped inside the cave. Captain Royal had evidently spent the night there, for his bed was even untidier than it had been the previous day.

"Perhaps he's gone fishing," said Frank.

He was looking about the cave and suddenly his gaze fell on a small cupboard, consisting of a box on a ledge of rock, in which he could see a number of books. He gave a low whistle of surprise.

"The worthy captain has a library," remarked Joe.

"Let's see what his taste in reading matter is like."

Frank went over to the improvised cupboard and picked up one of the books. It fell open and a number of strips of paper fluttered to the floor of the cave.

Frank bent to pick up the papers. He looked at them curiously.

"Newspaper clippings!"

"We might get a clue about him from them," Joe suggested.

In the dim light, Frank scrutinized one of the clippings. It was a despatch from Boston, dated several months previous, and consisted of an address on Egyptian civilization given by a world-famous traveler who had spoken in that city.

"This is uncommonly dull, if you ask me,"

said Frank at last, putting the clipping aside and picking up another.

"No mention of Todham Todd?"

"Not that I can find."

Joe took one of the other clippings and the boys perused them diligently, seeking some mention of the missing college professor.

All the clippings were devoted to various lectures that had been given by various speakers in different parts of the country within recent months.

"Looks as if he was a lecturer, or had some interest in lectures, at any rate," Joe commented.

Patiently, they examined clipping after clipping, but in none of them did they find any mention of Todham Todd. A further search of the cupboard, however, revealed a veritable mass of papers, and the boys settled down to a thorough study of them.

"He's a queer kind of sailor, that's sure," declared Frank. "I never heard of a sailor who collected clippings about lectures."

The other papers were similar clippings, as well as typewritten documents. When the boys examined these documents in the hope of finding some clue to the former activities of Captain Royal, they found that they were manuscripts of lectures on philosophy and other topics. But still they found no mention of the name of Todham Todd.

"Well, whether he's mentioned in these papers or not, I'm sure that Captain Royal and Todham Todd are the same man," observed Joe. "No sailor would ever carry all this stuff around with him."

"It certainly looks peculiar," his brother agreed. "But there are some more papers yet. We'll look through them all. If he is Todham Todd it's hardly likely that he would carry clippings about other men's lectures and none of his own."

Sheet after sheet, they perused. There were lectures by visiting authors, lectures by big-game hunters, lectures by Arctic explorers, lectures by college professors, photographs of lecturers.

"He is certainly interested in lecturing. Perhaps it's just a coincidence. Crazy men will do crazy things. Perhaps Captain Royal just has a sort of lunatic streak that way," said Joe finally, when it seemed evident that none of the clippings or documents bore any mention of Todham Todd.

"Perhaps you're right. I hate to admit it, though. I was sure we had stumbled on a red-hot clue."

Frank scrutinized the last of the clippings.

"Nothing about him in this one either. I can't figure it out. Beyond the fact that all these stories deal with lectures, there is no connection between them. They're all by different men and all on different subjects."

At that moment Joe espied a small box close by. He opened it, and out tumbled a second mass of clippings.

"Gee, look at this!" he exclaimed.

"More lectures?" questioned his brother, with a sigh.

"Lectures? No!" shouted the younger Hardy boy. "It's a murder case! Look, Frank!"

"You're fooling!"

But even as he spoke Frank Hardy scanned the sheet of newspaper his brother held towards him. There, in glaring headlines, were the words

BARTON BIXBY SHOT DOWN
Former Naval Officer Kills Old Friend
With a Shotgun
Police Follow Clues in Vain

There followed a long account of a killing that had taken place in Richmond three weeks before. A certain Lieutenant Patwick had murdered a former friend who had spoken ill of him at a club. Patwick had then fled to parts unknown. The lieutenant was said to be of a nervous, high-strung temperament.

"Gosh! he may not be Todham Todd after all," remarked Frank. "He may be this Lieutenant Patwick simply trying to conceal his true identity."

"Or else gone crazy because of his crime," added Joe.

There were several other clippings concerning the crime. Evidently the perpetrator had outwitted both police and detectives.

"We'll have to look into this," said Frank soberly.

"You bet. For all we know—"

Joe stopped speaking and thrust all the clippings behind him. A shadow had darkened the mouth of the cave.

"Who is in there?" an angry voice bellowed.

CHAPTER XX

The Shotgun

So QUIETLY had the man approached the cave mouth that the Hardy boys were taken completely by surprise. They wheeled about.

There, in the entrance, stood Captain Royal.

Evidently, it took him some time to become accustomed to the dim light of the cave, for he was peering intently at the boys, but with no sign of recognition on his face.

"Who's that?" he shouted impatiently. "Answer me!"

Frank gulped. Then, trying to achieve a confident tone of voice, he said:

"Why, hello, Captain. We just dropped in for a visit."

But Captain Royal was not appeased.

With a roar of wrath, he advanced into the cave.

"I know you now!" he bellowed. "I know you. It's those boys who were here yesterday. Don't deny it!"

"Sure!" said Joe. "It's only us."

The captain came closer.

"What are you doing in my place?" he demanded. "Stealing, eh?"

"We're not stealing," returned Frank indignantly.

"Yes, you are!" Captain Royal was plainly angry. "You came here to steal all my money and my jewels. I know it! You waited until I went out and then you sneaked in here to rob me."

"Now, Captain, be reasonable," pleaded Frank. "We just came here to have a little talk with you. If we wanted to steal we would have cleared out long ago."

"You came to steal!" insisted the old man. "Don't tell me anything different. Why can't you leave an old man alone? I've never done you any harm."

"Certainly not. We had no intention of disturbing you—"

Just then Captain Royal caught sight of the mass of clippings and papers. His face was suddenly distorted with fury.

"My papers!" he shrieked. "You've been at my papers!"

He made a sudden lunge toward the boys. So quickly did he rush at them that neither Frank nor Joe had a chance to escape. Captain Royal grasped each lad by the collar.

"You've been at my papers! My precious

papers! I knew you came here to steal some-thing!"

He shook them roughly.

"I'll teach you to come prowling around my cave!" he roared. "I will teach you to look at my papers."

The Hardy boys struggled to free themselves, but Captain Royal was stronger than he looked, and he kept a tight grip on their collars. Frank almost wriggled free, but the captain tightened his grasp. As for Joe, he told his chums later that "the old lad shook me until my back teeth rattled."

The captain was raging and roaring almost incoherently in a terrible outburst of wrath. There was now little doubt in the minds of the Hardy boys that the man was a lunatic. What would happen to them at the hands of this madman?

At first they had not taken Captain Royal's outburst seriously, but now Frank realized that they might be in genuine danger.

He lashed out with his fists and dealt the captain a blow in the ribs that brought a startled grunt. At the same time, Joe wriggled to one side and tried to trip the old gentleman. But Captain Royal was alert and wary. He would not let go, and although he lost his balance and tumbled to the floor of the cave, he dragged the boys with him.

"Break loose, Joe!" shouted Frank. "He means business."

But this was more easily said than done.

The trio sprawled on the floor of the cave, Frank and Joe fighting desperately to get out of the clutches of their captor, but the old man clung to their collars like grim death.

"I'll teach you!" he panted. "I'll shoot both of you."

His words sent a thrill of fear through the boys. They knew now that they were dealing with a maniac and they realized that in his present frame of mind, he was quite capable of carrying out the threat.

Joe had fallen in such a way that his collar had become twisted, and with Captain Royal still grasping it, he was almost choked. He could not turn without increasing the throttling pressure, so he was quite helpless. As for Frank, in spite of his struggles, he was unable to break the captain's hold.

"I have the better of you!" chuckled the old man fiendishly. "You can't get away from me. Try to kill me, would you! I'm going to shoot you both."

He began to struggle to his feet.

Captain Royal was eying something on the wall at the back of the cave. Following the direction of his gaze, Frank saw something that terrified him.

It was a double-barreled shotgun!

"I've got it loaded to the muzzle!" roared Captain Royal, as he floundered about in his efforts to get to his feet without losing his grip on the boys. "I've always kept it loaded just for prying thieves that come to steal my papers."

He stood up and lurched across the cave, dragging the boys with him. His intention was clear. He meant to get the shotgun.

The lads redoubled their efforts to escape. By a concerted effort, they turned on him, striking at him with their fists. Frank heard a ripping, tearing sound and then he was suddenly free. He staggered back, and the captain was left holding a small fragment of his shirt in his hand.

Frank thought quickly. He must reach the gun first. He leaped across the cave.

But Captain Royal was too quick for him. Flinging Joe to one side so that he went stumbling and then sprawled in the sand, the captain reached the shotgun at a bound.

He was just reaching for it when Frank came at him from behind. Captain Royal tried to fend the boy off, but Frank grappled with him and dragged him away from the wall.

"Get the gun, Joe!" he panted.

Joe was just getting to his feet. Captain Royal whirled about. His fist struck Frank

against the side of the head, and it caught
Frank off balance. He was knocked off his
feet. Captain Royal gave a yell of triumph,
and seized the shotgun.

It had been resting on a rocky ledge. Frank
was sprawled on the sand, entirely at the man's
mercy. Joe was equally helpless. In another
moment they expected to hear the explosive
roar of the weapon.

"Now, I'll teach you!" roared the captain,
dancing about in fury. "I'm going to shoot
the pair of you."

Frank had a sudden idea.

"I'll keep him occupied, Joe," he said in a
low voice. "Keep edging back until you get to
the cave mouth."

A daring plan had formed in his mind. It
meant, as he thought, risking his own life, but
he was prepared to do this for the sake of his
younger brother.

If he could but distract Captain Royal's attention by taunts and jeers, even if it meant
arousing the man to a pitch of murderous mad-
ness, Joe might make good his escape.

"You wouldn't have the nerve to shoot," he
shouted.

Captain Royal brandished the shotgun and
glared at Frank.

"I wouldn't have the nerve, hey? You think
I haven't?"

Joe was moving back, step by step, toward the opening.

"No, you wouldn't shoot me," scoffed Frank. "I don't believe your old gun is loaded anyway."

Captain Royal had forgotten all about Joe by now.

"Not loaded?" he screeched. "It's loaded to the muzzle, I tell you. It's always loaded. You'll find out if it's loaded or not."

Frank was preparing to spring to his feet.

"Listen, Captain Royal," he said placatingly. "Let me go this time and I promise I won't bother you again."

But the captain shook his head.

"You're a spy!" he screeched. "You're a spy! You were sent here to look through all my papers. I'm an old sailor, I am, and in the navy we have only one cure for spies."

"And what's that?"

"We shoot 'em." Captain Royal brandished the shotgun viciously. "We shoot 'em when we can't make 'em walk the plank."

"You haven't the nerve to shoot me. You wouldn't dare. You know you'd be hanged."

Frank glanced toward the mouth of the cave. Joe was almost safe by now.

"I'm not afraid!" bragged Captain Royal. "They'd never catch me to hang me. Death for the spies. I'll shoot both of you—"

Only then did he become aware that Joe had disappeared. With a growl of alarm, he swung about, just in time to see Joe vanishing beyond the cave mouth.

"He's gone!" roared the captain. "Come back here, you young scoundrel! Come back!"

He ran across the cave. Frank seized the opportunity to leap to his feet again. Captain Royal heard him and turned, raising the shotgun to his shoulder.

"You won't escape me!" he yelled.

The shotgun was leveled directly at the boy. Frank thought that the next moment would be his last. He could see Captain Royal's finger tightening about the trigger.

But there came an interruption from the mouth of the cave. Joe had heard the uproar and had realized his brother's danger. He had not fled. He had returned to the entrance, and there he gave vent to a shrill, blood-curdling shriek.

Captain Royal gave a shout of surprise.

"Who's that?" he exclaimed.

He whirled hastily about, but Joe had disappeared.

"Who's there?" he roared.

Joe, hidden beyond the rocks, shrieked again.

"Just wait!" yelled the captain. "I'll come out there and fix you. I'll fix you!"

Frank, in the meantime, had been circling

about the side of the cave, trying to gain the entrance unobserved. His heart sank as Captain Royal turned around just when he was about to make a dash for liberty.

"So!" yelled Captain Royal. "You thought you could get away from me, eh?"

The shotgun was aimed directly at Frank.

Captain Royal fired. There was a loud explosion.

CHAPTER XXI

OVER THE CLIFF

To FRANK HARDY's unbounded astonishment, the explosion was followed by a white cloud that rose from the barrel of the shotgun. It was not smoke, and although Captain Royal had aimed the gun directly at him, he found that he was uninjured.

The white cloud was flour!

"A hit!" roared Captain Royal. "A hit! I've wounded him!"

Frank wasted no further time.

He raced toward the mouth of the cave and scrambled out onto the beach. Behind him he could hear Captain Royal screeching wildly.

Frank almost collided with Joe.

His brother's face was white. He had heard the shot and was sure Frank had been a victim of the maniac's wrath.

"Are you all right, Frank?"

"Sure. Come on—let's beat it out of here."

They stumbled across the rocks toward a great heap of boulders that offered shelter.

Frank glanced back in time to see Captain Royal emerge from the cave, still carrying the shotgun.

"Did he miss you?" panted Joe.

Frank chuckled.

"If that gun had been loaded, my goose would have been cooked by now."

"But I heard the shot."

"It was loaded to the muzzle with flour. That's all. Just plain, ordinary flour."

They dropped down behind the boulders.

When they peeped out again they could see Captain Royal at the mouth of the cave, dancing with rage. Evidently he saw them, for he yelled:

"You can't hide from me. I can see you."

He raised the shotgun to his shoulder again and pressed the trigger. Once more there was a shower of flour distributed in every direction.

"Whether he's Todham Todd or Captain Royal, he's a lunatic," declared Joe.

"There's no question of that."

The boys crouched behind the boulder and watched the antics of the captain. He was yelling and shrieking like a wild Indian, waving the shotgun on high. Both barrels had been discharged.

"My ammunition is gone!" he roared. "My ammunition is gone!"

He hurled the gun away from him. It fell
with a clatter among the rocks.

Hatless and coatless, he was a weird figure
in the fog. He made no move toward the
Hardy boys, however, but contented himself
with dancing about at the mouth of the cave.

"The battle is lost!" shrieked Captain
Royal finally. "On to the execution!"

"What on earth does he mean?" said Joe.

"Oh, he's crazy, that's all. He doesn't mean
anything."

"All is lost! My enemies are upon me! On
to the execution! On to the execution!"

Captain Royal whirled about and ran down
the beach through the lowering mist.

"Where is he going?"

"Let's wait and watch him," advised Frank.

They saw the queer old man running and
stumbling among the rocks along the shore.
Then he turned to his right and began to
clamber up among the boulders until he came
to a scarcely visible path that led up toward the
top of the cliff.

From the boulders among which the Hardy
boys were standing they could scarcely see the
man now, so they emerged and went down
toward the cave. Captain Royal, yelling at the
top of his lungs, was climbing on up the path.

"What's his idea, anyway?"

Frank shook his head.

"He's certainly running amuck! I hope he doesn't fall and hurt himself."

The path the captain had taken wound about in precarious fashion and at one point crossed a ledge of rock that overhung the beach, immediately over the rocks that sloped down into the deep water.

Captain Royal stumbled and fell, but he got to his feet again and went on.

"If he ever slips when he comes to that ledge, he'll go over the cliff!" Joe declared.

"I wonder if we should follow him."

At that moment, the Hardy boys saw two figures come into view from beyond the rocks. At that distance and through the mist it was impossible to distinguish their features, but as they drew closer the Hardy boys saw that they were none other than Chet and Biff.

"What's going on here?" shouted Chet, as they hastened up.

"Lots of excitement," Frank replied. "Captain Royal has just had a brainstorm."

"What happened?"

When their chums came near, the Hardy boys told them of their adventures of the morning, how they had captured Carl Schaum, and how Captain Royal had come upon them while they were in the cave.

"And he shot at you?" cried Biff.

"With his gun loaded with flour."

"Flour?"

"Yes."

"He must be crazy."

"Absolutely."

"Where is he going now?"

Joe pointed to the captain, scrambling on up the path toward the cliff.

"There he is. And if he doesn't watch out he's going to tumble off into the sea."

"I'll say he is," declared Chet. "We ought to go after him."

In the distance, they could hear the wild shrieks of Captain Royal as he went stumbling among the rocks. He was drawing nearer to the ledge, and as the path at this point was extremely narrow, the boys could see that he was indeed in danger.

"Stop!" shouted Joe. "Stop, Captain!"

But Captain Royal, if he heard at all, paid no attention to the warning. He continued his ascent of the rocky path.

"We'd better follow him up," said Frank. "He can't hurt us—we know that—and he's sure to hurt himself if we don't get him down off those rocks."

With one accord, the boys hurried across the beach until they came to the trail leading up the steep incline toward the top of the cliff. Then, with Frank Hardy in the lead, they began the climb.

Captain Royal turned and saw them. He stopped and shook his fist at them.

"Go back!" he shouted wildly. "Go back, I tell you!"

"Come down!" called Frank. "Come down, Captain Royal, or you'll be killed."

"The battle is lost!" howled the madman. "My enemies are upon me! But they'll never capture me alive!"

He bent down and lifted a heavy stone, which he hurled down the path. It came rolling and bouncing down the slope, gathering momentum every second. It was headed directly for the Hardy boys and their chums.

"Scatter!" shouted Joe.

The boys had little protection. The path was so narrow that they could go neither to right nor left for more than a few inches.

On came the heavy stone.

The boys crouched, listening to the crash and clatter of the great missile as it bounded toward them. There was no use attempting to escape. If they ran back down the path they could never hope to reach the shore in time. The rock was plunging down the path at terrific speed. It seemed that the deadly object would crash among them in another moment.

Frank closed his eyes. Just then the rock bounded high in the air, shot forward in a wide arc, lit in the path just a few yards above the boys, and struck a projecting stone. It flew off at a tangent, the impact diverting it from its course so that it plunged wide of the boys who were crouched in the path. A moment later there was a tremendous crash as the heavy rock struck the beach.

Captain Royal, on the cliff above, was yelling with glee.

"You won't chase me now!" he shrieked. "That will teach you a lesson! That will teach you something!"

Frank scrambled to his feet. He was white with anger. The maniac's action had endangered their lives.

"We'll teach *you!*" he shouted. "Don't do a trick like that again. Come down off those rocks before you fall and break your neck."

"I won't come down."

Captain Royal shook his fist at them again, wheeled about and then continued his perilous climb. The boys hastened in pursuit. They knew that the old man might turn and cast another rock down the path, but they were determined to save him from the consequences of his own folly if they could.

The fog had left the rocks and the path slippery and treacherous. At almost every step the boys stumbled. It was almost impossible to maintain one's footing as the path grew steeper. As for Captain Royal, he was no better off, and more than once he went sprawling on all fours, only to pick himself up again and resume his hazardous progress.

At last he reached the top of the cliff.

The boys were still ¬any yards from the summit. Captain Royal made no attempt at caution as he ran along the narrow path. The rocks were slippery under foot.

"He'll go over, as sure as fate!" exclaimed Frank.

Scarcely were the words out of his mouth when the boys saw Captain Royal stumble. He lurched sideways, his arms thrashed the air as he vainly grabbed for support, he gave a desperate yell. The boys gave a simultaneous cry of terror as they saw the man plunge through the air, over the side of the cliff, down toward the water far below!

CHAPTER XXII

In Swirling Waters

THE boys looked at one another in awe.

Their ears still rang with Captain Royal's last dreadful cry as he went hurtling over the cliff toward the watery depths.

"He's gone!" gasped Chet. "I knew something like that would happen. He slipped on the rocks."

Frank, however, was already slipping and stumbling back down the path toward the beach.

"There's still a chance," he shouted to the others. "He may be alive yet. If we hurry we may be able to get him out of the water before he drowns. The tide's coming in, so he may be washed ashore."

It was a slim chance, he knew. Captain Royal had fallen from a great height and perhaps the impact of his collision with the water had rendered him unconscious. From the path, the boys could not see where the old man had

177

struck the water, so they could not know if he had come to the surface as yet.

The boys scrambled down the path, almost risking their necks in the pellmell descent. Rocks and pebbles went skittering before them as they plunged toward the beach.

All their resentment against Captain Royal because he had hurled the rock at them and because he had threatened them, had vanished in their concern for his safety. They realized that he was not responsible for his actions and that his eccentricities were the fruits of a disordered mind. They had done their best to save him from going over the cliff. This was some consolation. But the very thought of such a horrible death made them shudder.

"He'll be battered to pieces on the rocks!" panted Joe.

"If we get there in time we may be able to save him," returned Frank. "Of course, it's ten chances to one that he was killed by the fall."

They reached the rocks of the shore at last, Frank and Joe in front, Chet and Biff stumbling breathlessly along behind. The boys raced down the beach toward the base of the cliff from which Captain Royal had fallen. It was invisible to them from where they were, but as they skirted a ledge of rock they saw the steep wall of the precipice.

It descended to a raging foam of angry waters, where the surf beat among the black pinnacles of rock projecting from the sea at the base of the cliff.

"He hasn't a chance in the world," declared Chet, when he viewed the gloomy scene.

Fog hung over the shore, and through it loomed the black cliff and the cruel rocks. They could see no sign of Captain Royal in the waves.

However, the boys hastened on toward the base of the cliff, approaching as near as they dared. Frank scanned the water in vain for a glimpse of a bobbing figure being cast in toward the shore.

"He wouldn't live ten seconds in that sea!" declared Biff, with conviction.

"I'm afraid you're right, Biff," replied Frank sadly. "I guess we'll never see the poor old chap again."

"Pretty tough," said Chet. "After all, he didn't know what he was doing. He was just crazy. He should have been somewhere in a place where his friends could look after him."

"And now," put in Joe, "we'll probably never know if he was Todham Todd or not."

Chet looked up, interested.

"What's that?" he asked.

But before Joe could explain further, Frank gave a shout of excitement.

"I see him! Look!"

He pointed toward the black rocks at the base of the cliff. There, in the midst of the tossing waves, they had a momentary glimpse of a limp figure, an upturned face among the dark waters. There was no doubt that this was Captain Royal, but whether he was alive or dead they could not tell.

A gigantic wave picked up the body and hurled it toward the dark rocks again. Somehow, the limp form was thrown clear, otherwise it would have been battered to pieces, and it tumbled into a quiet pool beyond the jagged pinnacles. There the body lay, face upward, arms flung helplessly out.

"We've got to get him out of that," declared Frank, taking off his coat.

"How can we?"

"You'll be smashed to pieces against the rocks!" exclaimed Biff.

"I'm going to risk it anyway."

"You'd better wait for low tide."

"Too late then."

"Frank, don't be foolish!" cried Joe, in alarm. "You'll never be able to make it."

But Frank was obdurate.

"I can reach him if I'm careful," he said. "Perhaps he isn't dead. He may be only stunned and unconscious. If we leave him there he will be killed."

"But if he's dead already there's no sense in your risking your life."

"But he may not be dead. I'm going to try it, anyway."

Without another word, Frank handed his coat to Chet and then made his way along the rocks at the base of the cliff. For a few yards his progress was uneventful, but as he reached the deep water and the great waves pounded against him he was obliged to exert all his strength to breast the angry surf.

Once he was knocked off his feet and the watchers had a glimpse of his head and outflung arms in a smother of foam, then he disappeared from sight. A moment later, however, they saw him emerge, dripping, beside a rock that jutted out of the water and pull himself up to safety.

He still had a perilous journey before he could reach the limp form at the base of the rocky wall. He rested for a moment, with waves breaking over him as he clung to the rock. Then the watching boys saw him slip down into the water again and flounder on.

"He'll be battered to pieces!" exclaimed Biff.

"I wouldn't give a nickel for his chances, myself," said Chet.

Joe shook his head.

"He may get there all right, but if he tries

to bring Captain Royal's body back with him, he hasn't a Chinaman's chance."

Frank was now but a few yards away from the shallow pool where the old man lay. He vanished for a moment, emerged from the waves, staggered a few paces, then a huge roller swept over him and sent him against the side of the cliff. But he was evidently unhurt, for the others saw him wave toward them. Then he plunged along the base of the wall, flattened himself against the cliff as another wave rolled down upon him, and then splashed into the little pool.

"He made it!"

"Yes. But can he get back?"

Frank was bending over the body of Captain Royal. The other boys saw him straighten up suddenly and wave to them. He shouted something but the roar of the waves drowned his voice.

"Perhaps he's trying to tell us the captain is alive," suggested Joe.

They saw Frank tugging at the limp form, trying to get a convenient grip on Captain Royal's body.

"He's too heavy for Frank. It's hard enough for one person to get back through those waves alone, without dragging some one else along."

But evidently Frank was going to try it.

Going to the pool, his danger had been that a wave would pick him up and dash him to pieces against the rocks. Returning, his danger was that he would be unable to pit his strength against the force of the waves at all, that he would become exhausted before he reached the open shore again.

He had hoisted Captain Royal's body up until the old man's arms were over his shoulders, and he gripped the wrists over his chest. The body was thus across his back.

Head down, Frank plunged forward out of the sheltered pool, directly into the waves.

The first breaker smashed against him with terrific force. He lost his balance, staggered and fell. The watchers groaned. They saw the two figures in the foam, saw that Frank had lost his grip on Captain Royal.

But Frank managed to get to his feet. Then he reached out and seized the captain by the back of the shirt. He was not beaten yet.

He dragged the unconscious form into the very heart of the raging waves, where they surged against the sharp rocks. Each time a mighty roller came toward them, its crest tipped with foam, he lowered his head and set himself for the shock. So, inch by inch, he forged his way forward until he was among the rocks.

Here his danger was at its worst.

The water was not deep but a mistep would have grave consequences for if he once fell the waves would batter him against the rocks and his chances of regaining a foothold would be slim.

He rested a while in the shelter of the largest rock, waited until a huge wave went by with a crashing roar, then, as the water receded, plunged on again. Once he seemed to stagger, but he kept his balance, somehow, and clung to another rock.

Another wave came rolling in. Frank lowered his head and waited for it.

Crash!

It broke over him in a cloud of flying spray. He was completely hidden for a moment, and the watchers on the beach were breathless with suspense.

Then, through the mist, they saw that he was still clinging to the rock.

Frank was almost exhausted now. His burden, a dead weight, was very heavy. The beach seemed very far away. There were more rocks to pass. He rested for a short while, then plunged on.

By a miracle, he kept his footing among the treacherous rocks, and by good judgment he managed to get set in time to resist the shock of the breaking waves. At last he felt the sand beneath his feet.

He had only a short distance to go now, but his knees gave way beneath him. He stumbled and fell. He lost his grip on the body of Captain Royal. A great wave broke over them.

But Joe and Chet and Biff were already wading toward them. In a moment, Frank felt strong hands seizing him. Half-conscious, he was dragged out of the water onto the sands.

"Captain Royal!" he stammered. "Get him! He's all right!"

"Chet is bringing him in," said Joe assuringly.

"He's unconscious," gasped Frank, "but he's alive."

Then he collapsed, gasping and exhausted, on the sand. Chet came up, carrying the limp body of Captain Royal.

"He's breathing!" declared Chet excitedly. "Frank saved him."

CHAPTER XXIII

Back to Bayport

Captain Royal was unconscious, but he was still breathing. There was a bad cut on his head and it had bled profusely.

"We'd better get him to a doctor right away!" said Joe.

"I don't think he's been badly hurt." Chet began feeling the unconscious man's ribs. "There are no bones broken, at any rate. He hit his head against a rock, I guess."

"The blow on the head knocked him cold," Biff remarked.

"Perhaps he's got concussion of the brain."

"In that case, he needs a doctor," Joe said. "How about Frank?"

But Frank was already sitting up.

"I'm all right," he told them. "I'm just about all in, but I'll be as right as rain in a few minutes. Whew, those waves sure battered me about, I'll tell the world!"

"We never expected to see you come back alive," Chet told him.

186

"It was pretty bad coming back," Frank admitted. "The captain is heavier than he looks!"

"He's still alive, at any rate."

"Isn't he conscious yet?"

"Not a bit of it. He's breathing, but he's still dead to the world, and there's no sign that he's coming to."

"Well, we've got to get him to a doctor, that's all," declared Frank decisively.

He got to his feet, exhausted though he was.

"Do you mean that we'll carry him back to the road?" asked Joe.

"We'll take him right back to Bayport. That's where the nearest hospital is that we know anything about." Frank looked down at the unconscious man. "He's in bad shape. If he were just stunned, he'd be awake by now. Chances are, his skull is fractured. That's a bad cut."

The boys looked down at the unconscious Captain Royal, sprawled limply on the sand.

"It's a long haul," demurred Biff.

"We can't leave him here. We can't do anything for him ourselves, you know that."

"You're right." Biff bent over and grasped the unconscious man's feet. "Give me a hand with him, some one."

Chet and Joe helped him. They raised Captain Royal from the ground and began carrying him up the beach. Frank went on ahead, still weak from the effects of his grueling ordeal in rescuing the eccentric old man from the sea.

Captain Royal showed no signs of returning consciousness. He was a dead weight as the boys carried him on past his own cave, past the place where Carl Schaum had been hiding, past the boys' cave. There the lads rested, before undertaking the hard climb up the path to the top of the cliff.

They tried all the first aid measures they had ever heard of, but Captain Royal still remained unconscious. The cut on his head was not bleeding any more; his breathing was heavy, and the lads saw that it was no ordinary case of being rendered senseless by a blow on the head.

"A doctor is the only thing," declared Frank. "His lungs are clear of water, so he's all right in that respect. He must have struck his head when he was washed in among those rocks."

"Well, let's get busy then," said Biff, who was no laggard. "We had better get him to the hospital as quickly as we can."

They took turns carrying Captain Royal up the path that led to the top of the cliff. It was an arduous climb, and it was late in the afternoon before they finally reached the rocks above. Then they rested once more before starting the journey to the fisherman's cottage.

"Thank goodness, he has a car," said Joe. "He'll help us take him in to the city. We would never be able to carry him on the motorcycles."

"A queer end to our exploration trip," grunted Chet.

Puffing and panting, they carried the unconscious man on over the rocks until they came to the path leading down to the fisherman's cottage. There they rested again.

Finally, after a halting descent, they came to the cottage. Their friend, the fisherman, was fortunately at home. Accompanied by his wife, he came running out when the boys appeared in sight with their burden.

"First it's a prisoner and now it's a sick man!" he exclaimed, as he drew near. "I declare, you chaps seem to scare up more excitement than anybody that ever came to Honeycomb Caves."

"This is an old man who was living in one of the caves," explained Frank. "He fell off a cliff and hurt himself. Do you think you could help us get him to a doctor?"

The fisherman glanced inquiringly at his wife.

"Go ahead, John," she said. "You wouldn't let the poor man die, would you?"

"I wondered if you'd mind bein' left alone."

"Go on. I'm not a baby. Drive the poor fellow out to a doctor. It's easy to be seen he needs attention."

The fisherman quickly brought out his car and they carefully put Captain Royal in the back seat. The boys brought out their motorcycles and, with Biff riding in company of the fisherman, the little party set out for the main road.

"I don't know whether we can find a doctor at the village or not," said the fisherman. "If we can't, there's nothing for it but to drive on into Bayport."

"We'll fix the expenses," Frank assured him.

"That's all right. I don't want any money for my trouble. The poor old chap seems to have got a terrible wallop on the head. How did it happen?"

"He fell off a cliff."

"Did it have anything to do with the fellow you brought out this morning?" asked the fisherman shrewdly.

"No. Nothing to do with him."

They reached the main road and drove on toward the village. There they found that the one and only doctor had been called out on a case and would not be back until the following morning.

"Bayport it is, then," said Joe.

It was plain that the fisherman did not relish

"We're going back a lot quicker than we left," replied his brother.

At length they came within sight of the twinkling lights of Bayport. The roar of the big automobile did not diminish. At breakneck speed they clattered into the city limits.

In the back seat of the car, Biff turned frequently to look at the unconscious form beside him. To his relief, Captain Royal was still breathing.

"I think the old chap will pull through all right," he said to himself.

Up a dark, quiet street sped the car, then came to a stop before a massive stone house with a neat gilt plate beside the door. The motorcycles roared up and the boys dismounted.

"We'll take him in and let the doctor have a look at him," said Mr. Jacobson. "If he is in bad shape, the doc will put him in his own private hospital. He'll get the best of care here."

Carefully, they carried Captain Royal up the steps. Their ring was answered by a servant, and they took the old man into a waiting room. The doctor, who had been in bed, soon came downstairs in pyjamas and dressing gown.

"An accident case, Doctor," explained Frank. "This old man fell off a cliff into the sea and he's been unconscious for eight or nine hours."

The doctor made a swift examination. His frown deepened as he inspected the cut on Captain Royal's temple.

"Queer!" he said. "It isn't a very bad cut, and there seems to be no sign of a fracture. It looks like concussion of the brain, to me, but he doesn't appear to have had a very hard blow."

"The waves washed him up against the rocks," said Joe.

The doctor shook his head.

"He seems in a bad way. Eight hours, you said?"

"Yes."

"I'll have to give him a more detailed examination. I'll admit him as a patient to my own hospital if you people will be responsible for him."

"That's all right, Doctor. Do what you can for him and send the bill to us," said Frank promptly.

The doctor rang a bell. An attendant appeared, wheeling a long, white table. Captain Royal was placed upon it and wheeled away.

"I'll let you know in the morning," promised the doctor. "Frankly, I don't mind telling you he's in bad shape. He may never regain consciousness again."

The boys were sobered by the thought that Captain Royal, for all his eccentricities, might be dying as a result of his wild dash over the rocks. Slowly they filed out into the street, bade good-bye to Mr. Jacobson and thanked him for his assistance, then went home. As Chet Morton lived out in the country, the Hardy boys invited him to spend the rest of the night with them. He accepted the invitation gladly, for the prospect of a long trip out of the city had not appealed to him. Biff Hooper, who lived near by, went to his own home.

The house was in darkness when they arrived, so the Hardy boys and Chet quietly parked their motorcycles, slipped up the back stairs and were soon in bed. They were so tired after their adventures of the day that in spite of the temptation to discuss matters, sleep soon overcame them.

CHAPTER XXIV

At the Hospital

NEXT morning, refreshed by their sleep, Frank, Joe and Chet were downstairs early, but not earlier than Fenton Hardy, who was already busy in his office clearing up some work before breakfast. He welcomed them cheerily.

"Back so soon!" he exclaimed. "I thought this trip would keep you away at least a week. What's the matter? Did you get frightened by the sea serpent?"

"We didn't get frightened, Dad. We had to come back with a man who got hurt."

"Oh." Fenton Hardy's expression changed to one of concern. "Who is he?"

"We think he's Todham Todd."

"Todham Todd!" exclaimed the detective. "Are you sure?"

"We're not sure. But we have an idea that's who he is. And he may be a murderer too."

Mr. Hardy motioned the three boys to chairs. "Sit down and tell me all about it. A murderer! That sounds bad."

With Frank as spokesman, and Chet and Joe prompting him once in a while, they told Mr. Hardy about their meeting with Captain Royal, about the eccentric behavior of the old man and of his actions on finding the brothers looking over the clippings in the cave, culminating in his fall from the cliff.

"And he's at the private hospital now," concluded Frank.

"Well," said Mr. Hardy, "we'll have breakfast now and then we can soon settle the matter once and for all. Evangeline Todd is staying at the summer hotel and we can ask her to come over to the hospital and have a look at this Captain Royal."

"Do you think he can be this Lieutenant Patwick, Dad?" asked Joe.

"Possibly. If so, the crime may have turned his mind. Such things have happened."

"Well, if he's Patwick then we'll have cleared up something anyway," remarked Frank.

Breakfast was announced a few minutes later, and after the Hardy boys had been warmly greeted by their mother they sat down to fruit, bacon and eggs, toast and coffee and jam, to which they did full justice. They were anxious, however, to call on Miss Todd.

Mr. Hardy called up the private hospital and inquired about Captain Royal. He came back, his face serious.

"The old chap is still unconscious. The doctor seems to think he has only a slim chance."

"It will be tough if he turns out to be Todham Todd after all," said Joe. "Too bad if we've found him, only to have him die."

"Everything may turn out all right," said Mr. Hardy. "Of course he may not be Todham Todd. You have only your suspicions to go on, although I must say it's very strange that the old man should have had all those lecture clippings in the cave. I've been thinking that Todham Todd may have lost his memory and forgotten his identity. He may have had a dim recollection of once having been a lecturer of some kind so he took to collecting all the newspaper stories he could, in an effort to awaken his memory again."

"I'll bet you're right!" exclaimed Chet. "That sounds mighty reasonable to me."

"It's just a theory. Still, it may be true. We'll call on Miss Todd."

They left the house and went on down to the hotel at which Miss Evangeline Todd was staying. She had just concluded her breakfast when they arrived.

"Have you any news?" she asked quickly, when she recognized her visitors.

"We have news, of a sort," admitted Fenton Hardy.

"Tell me. What is it? Has Todham been

found? Is he well?'' Miss Todd sank back in
a chair and fanned herself with a magazine.
''Don't keep me in suspense.''

''We have found a man who may or may not
be your brother.''

''Where is he?'' demanded Miss Todd, getting up quickly. ''Take me to him at once?''

Mr. Hardy laid a restraining hand upon
her arm.

''Don't count on this too much, Miss Todd,''
he advised. ''This man may not be your
brother at all. As a matter of fact, we have
nothing definite to go on, but we'd like to have
you come with us and identify him if you can.''

''Identify him? Is he dead?''

''No. But he's in a local hospital.''

''Todham in a hospital? Where? I must go
to him at once.''

''Now, as I've already said, we're not at all
certain that this man is your brother. If you
will come with us we will show you this man
and you will be able to see for yourself if he is
your brother or not.''

''Just a minute, until I put on my hat. I'll
go with you right away. My goodness, if it's
really Todham—''

Talking to herself in her excitement, Miss
Todd bustled away upstairs and returned in a
few minutes, her hat awry.

''Hurry!'' she said. ''Where is the hospital?

We'll take a taxi and get there more quickly."

Fenton Hardy smiled sympathetically. Miss Todd was tremendously agitated at the prospect of again seeing her long-lost brother. The hospital was less than three blocks away, so they did not hail a taxi after all, but walked the short distance, and in a little while they found themselves in the doctor's waiting room.

A uniformed nurse entered.

"You want to see the patient called Captain Royal?"

"If you please."

"The doctor is with him now, but he says you may go up. I will show you to his room."

"Captain Royal!" exclaimed Evangeline Todd. "That isn't his name! I thought you said he might be my brother."

"That is the name he has been using," explained Frank. "How is he this morning, nurse?"

"There isn't much change in his condition. The doctor says it is a strange case. But, I'm afraid—"

"Isn't he going to live?" asked Miss Todd sharply.

Fenton Hardy soothed her anxiety.

"Now, Miss Todd, try to calm yourself. We must be very quiet, you know. This man is very, very sick."

The lady heeded his advice. During the rest

of their journey down the long corridor she talked only in whispers. At length they reached the door of a private room. The nurse knocked. The boys heard the doctor's voice, saying, "Come!"

The nurse held open the door and they entered a spacious private room, spotlessly clean and well-lighted. Lying on the bed was Captain Royal, with a white bandage around his head.

Evangeline Todd looked at the man wildly, then rushed to the bedside.

"My brother!" she cried. "It's my brother, Todham!"

She leaned over the unconscious figure.

"Speak to me, Todham! Speak to me! Don't you recognize me? It's you're sister. I've hunted everywhere for you, and now I've found you at last."

Then, overcome with emotion, she sank beside the bed and burst into tears.

"It's the missing professor, after all!" exclaimed Chet, in awe.

The Hardy boys, while they had expected that Evangeline Todd would identify Captain Royal as her brother, were electrified with delight.

"We were right!" said Frank. "He was Todham Todd all along."

Mr. Hardy and the doctor tried to calm the

weeping woman, who was almost hysterical with relief, now that her long search was ended.

"It's Todham!" she said, over and over again. "It's my brother. I would know him anywhere."

But the man in the bed knew nothing of what was going on. His eyes were closed. His face was white and calm. Had it not been for an occasional slight twitching of the nostrils one might have thought that he was dead.

The doctor, who knew nothing of the reason for Miss Todd's outburst, was astonished, but in a few words Fenton Hardy explained the situation to him. He shook his head sadly.

"And this is where she has found her brother, at last?"

"Yes. He has been missing for months."

"I'm afraid," said the doctor, "that she has found him only to lose him."

"Is it that serious?"

"It's concussion of the brain, and there seem to have been complications. He has only a slim chance to live."

CHAPTER XXV

The Last of Captain Royal

Todham Todd hovered between life and death for almost two weeks. For days he lay unconscious, knowing nothing of the efforts that were being made to save him. He had the best of care, and the doctor gave him every attention, but admitted that the case was one in which he could do little.

"We simply have to wait," he told the Hardy boys and Miss Todd. "He may be restored to consciousness at any moment. On the other hand, he may die just as quickly. He has a good constitution, so we may at least hope for the best."

They were anxious days. Every morning, the Hardy boys called at the hospital to inquire about the strange patient, and every morning the answer was the same.

"Mr. Todd's condition is unchanged."

One morning Fenton Hardy came to his sons with a newspaper in his hand. He was smiling broadly.

"I think the mystery is explained," he said. "Read this."

In the newspaper was an account of the capture of Lieutenant Patwick. The man had been shot down on the seacoast by detectives. Thinking he was going to die, he had admitted the murder of Barton Bixby. He also spoke of hiding in a cave with a strange old man, a lunatic.

"Todham Todd," murmured Frank.

"That makes everything as clear as day," added Joe.

"He must have left his clippings with Captain Royal," said Mr. Hardy. "Murderers usually like to read all that is printed about their crimes."

The boys told Evangeline Todd the entire story of their meeting with Captain Royal, although in deference to the good lady's feelings they refrained from mentioning the fight in the cave or the incident of the shotgun. How Todham Todd had found his way down to the coast and what had prompted him to call himself Captain Royal and take up his hermit existence in the cave, were mysteries.

"If he recovers, he may remember nothing about that phase," the doctor had said. "You may use your own judgment whether to tell him of it or not."

"We shan't tell him," declared Evangeline

Todd decisively. "Let him take up the threads of his old life anew."

Then her face clouded.

"That is—if he recovers," she added, with a catch in her voice.

There came a morning when the nurse in charge saw the eyelids of the sick man flutter, and then he spoke.

"Where am I?" he asked, in a puzzled tone.

"You are quite safe," the nurse told him. "You have met with an accident. You are in the hospital."

"Ah, yes," he said. "I remember now. There was a railroad accident. Something must have struck me on the head. I can remember a sudden blow, and that is all."

"You have been unconscious for a long time, Captain. You must be quiet."

"Captain?" he said. "I'm not a captain. My name is Todd. My name is Todham Todd. I'm a professor at the university."

The doctor was called. He questioned the patient carefully and it was soon evident that Todham Todd had recovered his memory with the exception of the time following the first accident that had resulted in amnesia. From that time, everything was a blank. He knew nothing of his wanderings, knew nothing of what had happened in the caves, knew nothing of the accident that had restored his memory again.

"He will live," the doctor told Evangeline Todd a short time later. "His memory is completely restored. Unless complications set in, he should be able to leave the hospital within a few days."

The doctor's prediction was correct.

Todham Todd, completely restored in memory, was able to leave the hospital before the week was out. The reunion between the man and his sister was an affectionate one. The professor had not the slightest inkling of all the strange events that had transpired from the time of the first accident until he woke up in the hospital at Bayport. He was deeply puzzled when he learned where he was, but the doctor covered up his bewilderment by explaining that his case had been so unusual that he had been brought there for special treatment when the doctors of his home city had failed to bring him back to consciousness.

He was introduced to the Hardy boys by Miss Todd, who was pathetically grateful to the lads for restoring her brother to her, safe and sound again. But there was no sign of recognition. Seeing the boys struck no responsive chord in Professor Todd's memory. He knew nothing of the days when he had played at being Captain Royal. To all intents and purposes, he was seeing the Hardy boys for the first time.

They were content to let it remain at that and were careful to say nothing that might indicate they had known him previously. And when Todham Todd finally left the hospital and went to the hotel where his sister was staying, to rest there a few days before going back home, the Hardy boys were his firm friends.

"We must never let him know," said Evangeline Todd to the boys that evening.

"You may rely on us, Miss Todd," they assured her.

"I can't tell you how grateful I am," she said. "If you boys had not been shrewd enough to think that Captain Royal might be Todham Todd after all, things might not have turned out as they have. You might not have concerned yourselves with him any more, and he might still be living that wretched life in the caves. I want to reward your father and yourselves for finding him."

But Fenton Hardy had already expressed himself on the subject of the reward.

"I want nothing," he said. "You have already paid any expenses I incurred in trying to trace Mr. Todd. As for finding him, the credit belongs to the boys."

But the Hardy boys were insistent in their refusal.

"We're only too glad that we helped find him," they told Miss Todd. "We couldn't accept a reward for what we did. In a way, it was chance that threw him in our path.''

Although Miss Todd pleaded with them to alter their decision, they were firm.

''Our greatest reward is in seeing your brother with you again, with his memory restored,'' declared Frank. ''We want nothing more than that.''

But Miss Todd expressed her appreciation in tangible form before she left Bayport. She invited the Hardy boys and some of their chums, Chet Morton, Biff Hooper, Phil Cohen, Tony Prito, Jack Dodd and Jerry Gilroy, to a banquet at the hotel, and there the lads sat down to a ''spread'' the like of which they had not seen before. There was everything dear to the heart of a boy, from fried chicken, fluffy mashed potatoes and sweet pickels, to ice-cream and five different kinds of pie.

Professor Todham Todd, white-haired, kindly-faced, looking quite different from the wild-eyed Captain Royal of Honeycomb Caves, presided at the banquet and made a little speech in which he thanked them all for their interest in his welfare and their kindness to him. Although he had no idea of the real part the Hardy boys and their chums had played in his recovery, he had taken a genuine liking to them and it is probable that he enjoyed the banquet as much as any one.

When the lads had eaten of chicken and ice-cream until they could eat no more, Miss Todd stood up and said she had an announcement to make.

"You all know something of the circumstances under which we have gathered here to-night. You all know the debt of gratitude I owe to the Hardy boys, in particular, and to Chet Morton and Biff Hooper. So if they will stand up, I have something for them."

Blushing, the four lads got to their feet.

"All I can say," continued Miss Todd, "is that my brother and I thank you very, very much."

Todham Todd looked a bit bewildered, but he smiled quite as though he knew what it was all about. It was probable that the good man was mildly puzzled until the end of his life as to the reason for the presentations.

For Miss Todd thereupon handed Frank and Joe an order for a handsome motion picture camera, something they had long wished to own. To Chet and Biff she gave each a gold watch and chain.

"Speech! Speech!" shouted the other boys, as the recipients of the gifts stammered their thanks.

After considerable pressure, Frank was at last prevailed upon to say a few words.

"I'm not a very good orator," he said.

"You're a better detective," shouted one of the lads at the table.

Perhaps he was—and Joe, too. One can decide in "The Mystery of Cabin Island."

"I'm not a very good orator," Frank said, "but I certainly want to thank Miss Todd very much indeed, although we don't deserve such a beautiful present."

There were loud cheers for this effort, as the boy sat down blushing.

"Speech from Chet Morton!"

"Say, listen—" protested the bashful Chet. But he was shoved to his feet.

"Speech! Chet Morton's going to make a speech!"

"Gosh, I can't say anything except that I thank Miss Todd very much and I'm glad Professor Todd is well again and—and I wonder if there's to be a second helping of ice-cream."

There was.

THE END